THE OPEN BOOK

THE OPEN BOOK

L. MARIE WOOD

FALSTAFF
BOOKS
WWW.FALSTAFFBOOKS.COM

For SAW, BKW, and MDW – always.

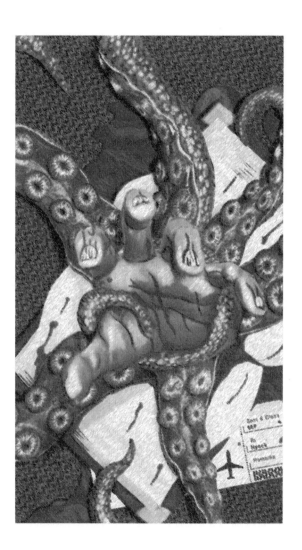

PROLOGUE

THE TENTACLES HAD BARELY TUCKED themselves securely away before someone noticed the book lying open near the seat. The man had been the first one to ever resist, and his misstep proved delightful, at least for one of them; the other, not so much. Having the last thing ever seen in waking life be the gelatinous underbelly of a creature whose name can't quite be placed but that smells of the familiar, nonetheless; to know that the sound of sucking and slurping was the result of some other being's pure gastronomic ecstasy at the taste of one's own flesh; to understand, yet try to blot out the fact that one is breathing last breath number 5, then number 4, and so on, must have been hellacious. The effect was much like a tenderizer on tough meat; a sweet undertone of flavor infused in gracious quantity.

Innocent and tranquil lay the book, its pages open to the stale air of the airport terminal. There was no trace of the blood that had poured from the man's gaping mouth as his insides compressed, no residue from his eyes that had burst from the pressure. All of that had been carefully consumed, the contents fusing with the dexterous appendages as if animate themselves. There was nothing to see. Nothing to know. Its life was, indeed, an open book.

1

A WOMAN PULLING one of those wheeled carry-on bags approached. She was dressed elaborately, bright colors tangoing on her duster; knee-high boots adorning her calves and feet. She wasn't paying attention to where she was going —her smartphone possessed all her attention. Because of that, she stepped right onto the yellowed pages of the book and stumbled, surprised by the obstruction. The woman bent down to pick up the book and had every intention of placing it on a seat and continuing on. It was either that or kicking it under the chair, but that wouldn't be right, would it? It probably fell out of someone's bag, left there by a person who had already boarded their flight. Kicking it under the chair was wrong—that was littering, wasn't it? Wasn't she trying to do better about things like that? Wasn't the whole reason she was in the airport dragging environmentally conscious cleaning supplies around because she wanted to make a difference in the world? The woman frowned as much at the book on the floor as at the absurdity of her current situation (have toilet bowl cleaner, will travel) and picked up the book, deciding to take it to the people at the gate check-in counter. What they did with it then was up to them.

"I guess I'm doing my part," the woman said aloud to no one in particular. A little boy laying on his mother's lap stared at her as she reached for the book.

The woman pulled it toward her, noticing that it was open to a story. Her eyes cascaded over the page, reading the first few sentences before she realized what she was doing.

Home Party

You gotta be kidding me.

The front of the trailer was barely visible beneath the overgrown bushes, if they could even be called bushes. They looked like the stuff that grows at the base of trees, wispy and vine-like, with pathetic little leaves that were more brown than green. They covered the front of the trailer in clumps, all camo green and switch bearing, growing wild. Where there weren't bushes, there were bins of empty beer cans. Four of them on the splintered porch and at least three in the tall grass that made up the yard. The place stank of beer, piss, and sweat.

THE CORNUCOPIA of sound from the loudspeakers filled the woman's ears in a rush. She bolted upright as if she had received an electric shock. Her head whipped from side to side, her eyes desperately searching for something, but not finding purchase. Then as they landed on the little boy who stared at her from his mother's lap, the child whose eyes seemed to take up most of his face, she settled down. He pointed at the pool of urine that had formed below her. She felt the warm path it had traced along her leg before hitting the floor, felt her pants sticking to her. She looked at the puddle, the strangest smile forming at the corners of her lips.

In silence, the woman walked to her gate and got in line with the other passengers, cracking the book open as she did.

CARRIE LOOKED AT THE PLACE, *noting that two of the windows facing the front of the house were boarded up, and the window in what might be the kitchen was so tiny, it was hard to see into. But was someone looking out? She looked around the yard. Given the state of the house, she expected there to be a bunch of discarded, rusted out cars littering the lawn, but that cliché didn't fit. There was an older model Ford, but aside from faded paint and an ancient dent on the passenger side, it had been kept up. There was a sticker in the back window from the local college. There was also a brand new pickup truck. All this was odd, but not that odd. They could have needed a pickup for work and maybe it wasn't really new... just new to them. The Ford made total sense—a college student paying for something herself. You get what you need. That explained the beer cans too, and maybe even the boarded-up windows. One party with college kids could produce half the number of bottles in those bins. And what's a good college party without a broken window?*

But as she sat in the car, trying to rationalize everything she was seeing, she didn't believe it. The trailer didn't feel like a college hangout or a hauler's dive to crash in when he wasn't working long hours. It felt... wrong. It felt empty, but not because no one lived there. It felt lost.

Carrie swallowed, her mouth going dry while thoughts of crazy hill people of Texas Chain Saw Massacre *variety ran through her head. She forced a self-deprecating smile and got out of the car. It's no mansion, but it's someone's house, she told herself, and allowed for a hint of reproach to show in her inner voice. She had never* been one to judge a book by its cover, as the saying goes, and she wasn't going to allow herself to start now. She straightened her smart blazer, red for the season and a perfect accompaniment to the new product line she toted with her to this afternoon's soirée. She has been excited about showing the new bags to this group of people. The lottery she posted in the local nail salon gave her entrants who wanted to have a home party and look at the new catalog items. Michele Davenport, resident at this trailer, was the lucky winner. After weeks of excited conversations, party day was here. And alone in the gravel driveway of a broken down trailer stood Carrie.

It was quiet for mid-afternoon.

Carrie got back in the car, suddenly spooked. She looked at her watch. 1:30. She was supposed to be there a half an hour early and she was late. She got stuck behind Sunday drivers on the two-lane road leading to the place and got there with only ten minutes to set up. And she ate half of that time up staring at the trailer.

Maybe there was no one there. If there was, surely, they would have heard her car idling, would have seen her sitting there. As annoying as that would be (driving 45 minutes to get stood up was not her idea of a fun afternoon), Carrie didn't really want to go in the trailer. In fact, she thought, come hell or high water, I'm not getting in the trailer. There was something in the trailer that she didn't want to see. Something that was watching her, waiting for her to knock on the door, to look too closely at that little window in what might have been the kitchen. She could almost hear it breathing; a wet, phlegmy sound that made her skin crawl. And it was watching her. It had been watching her the whole time.

Carrie turned the car on and put it in gear without looking back at that window. She didn't see the front door open, didn't see the college student's odd, slow gait toward the car. She didn't see what trailed behind her, coloring the high grass. Carrie threw her arm over the passenger seat to back out of the driveway, but a car parked her in. Laughing ladies in the front seat smiled at her, *excited about the party, the games, the goodies. She didn't see the larger of the two lick her fingers as she pulled herself out of the car.*

THE FLIGHT ATTENDANT noticed the book laying open when she moved through the cabin after the passengers had disembarked, the pages facing the seat. She sighed, irritated that there never seemed to be a flight where people just did as they were told. Take all your stuff with you when you leave. Do not leave wadded up napkins containing god knows what in the seatback in front of you. Do not stuff garbage between the cushions or leave things behind. Seems simple, but there was always something left.

She picked up the book and prepared to throw it out, already catching a glimpse of sandwich wrappers and—what is that, chewed up gum?—wedged under the window shade, but the cover caught her attention. The intricate design, elegant and ornate, was breathtaking. The lettering appeared to be gold done in the finest calligraphy. *The Tales of Time.* A smile played at the corners of her mouth as she imagined a fragrant wind mussing her hair as she stood on a beach with the book in her hand. She could almost feel the breeze cooling her skin; could almost smell the ocean air as if she stood directly on its shores. She opened her eyes to look at the cover again, not realizing she had closed them.

The Tales of Time.

The wonderfully winding lettering reached up like vines to caress her skin. She inhaled luxuriantly, the memory of the sea making the moment surreal. With a decisive grunt, she put the book into her apron.

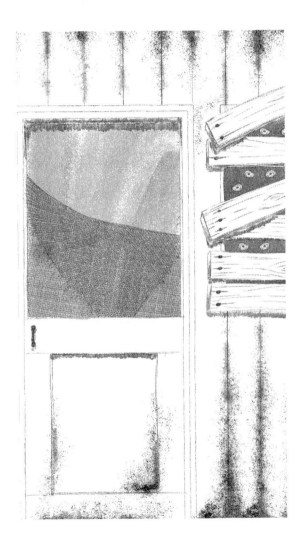

2

THE FLIGHT ATTENDANT walked into the coffee shop near her house and sighed at what she saw. The line was almost to the door. She shook her head and leaned out to look at the barista, a young girl with purple streaks in her hair and a discreet little nose ring that was still visible even though she probably thought it was concealed. The other two people behind the counter were working frantically in a cloud of froth and steam, the look of barely-contained panic showing on their faces.

This could take a while.

She put her hand into her bag to pull out her phone, and it brushed against the book she had found on the seat of the plane. She took the book out and examined the cover again.

The Tales of Time.

She felt windswept all over again as she opened it and thumbed through the front matter, looking for nothing in particular, but noticing that there was nothing to find either. No dedication page; no copyright page. No author name listed anywhere. Just blank, yellowed paper.

The line moved.

Her brow furrowed as she stepped forward to keep up.

When she found the first page of type, she breathed a sigh of relief. She had been holding her breath without realizing it, afraid the pretty little book she found was really just a journal some wannabe introspective passenger left behind. But no, the book had words and lots of them. She flipped through it as she stepped forward; another sweet and foamy drink delivered to a happy customer. There were several short stories inside. She turned back to the beginning of the book in search of a table of contents to see if any titles jumped out at her, but there was none to be found.

"Humph," she said under her breath. The guy in front of her turned, doing that passive-aggressive thing we are all guilty of—the one where we turn to the side like something important is happening over there but really we are glaring at the person behind us out of the corner of our eyes—showing her his chiseled profile and a mildly disapproving expression to go along with it. She couldn't help but thinking that he would be really hot if he would dislodge the stick that had wedged itself in his ass so firmly. She smiled at him coyly, thinking she'd happily help him with that, if he wanted.

The line moved.

She stepped forward, almost banging the book into pretty boy's back.

She leaned out to see how many more people were in front of her: four.

Great.

She started reading.

Impure

He sat in the shadows watching her as she moved, savoring the way the light caught the red in her hair, the way her chin dipped slightly to the left as she thought. He was tempted—that went without saying. But it went beyond the innate desire to satisfy the burning in his lap. Indeed, his hand resting there, absently stroking, was far removed from his thoughts. Instead he spoke to her, told her exactly what he wanted to do to her. He caressed the words, leaving them silky and smooth. He reached for her and felt her rise to meet his—

"Miss?"

The flight attendant looked up from the book in a daze. She felt hot, flushed, like she had been running, or...

"Ma'am, do you know what you want?"

The flight attendant looked at the barista waiting impatiently behind the counter. The line had depleted, and she was next. She was still standing yards away from the counter, where she had been when she started reading. Surprised, she looked back at the barista.

"I-I-," she stammered.

"Do you need a minute to decide?"

"N-No. I know what I want."

She walked toward the counter. One, two, three strides. She caught sight of pretty boy waiting for his drink at the pick-up counter. The smirk he wore made him look even more appealing than before.

She smiled at the barista, ordered, turned on that charm she reserved for work, and diffused the situation. She paid awkwardly, fumbling with the book and the credit card and her purse and her phone and all the crap that ended up in her hands as she stood at the counter. Laughing self-deprecatingly, as the situation called for, she put everything on the counter, the book included, which she did reluctantly.

'A woman fitting the description was seen driving the car toward Eel Road in a rural Virginia neighborhood this morning, sources say...'

The flight attendant heard the news in the background.

She gathered up her things not realizing that her mind was picking out bits and pieces of the news story to focus on. Eel Road Didn't she know where Eel Road was? Maybe. Maybe not.

'... the body was discovered by a neighbor who didn't recognize the car...'

The flight attendant turned to the screen to look at the news story rather than listen to it.

'... we heard somebody knocking on the door, but nobody's lived there in years.'

"Ma'am? You can pick up your drink at the pickup at the end of the counter."

The flight attendant looked at the purple-haired barista who was clearly losing patience with this distracted routine. She flashed another winning smile, grabbed her purse, and went to the pickup counter, where her drink was already waiting for her.

Pretty boy was gone.

It took her almost two hours to realize she had lost the book. After going to the gym, the cleaners, and the grocery store, she almost didn't care. Except she did. She wanted to know what happened with the weird stalker guy she was reading about. She wanted to feel the way she felt in line again, wanted the sensation of someone telling her what they wanted her to do… where they wanted her to touch…

The flight attendant called the coffee shop to ask about the book. She could almost hear the laughter in the girl's voice. It was Purple Hair, she was sure of it. Purple Hair thought it was funny that someone could be that desperate for a book that they would call about it like it was a precious jewel or something. How did she know the flight attendant was desperate, she wondered? Could it have been how fast she was talking when Purple Hair answered the phone? Maybe it was that harsh intake of breath when Purple Hair said the book was gone. Even more likely, Purple Hair heard the sadness that she couldn't keep out of her voice when she realized the name of the book had escaped her. Maybe it *was* funny. Maybe Purple Hair was right.

The flight attendant went online and researched the book, describing the cover the best she could, but the memory of it was hazy now. Was there water? A horse? Words on the cover? Sher couldn't remember—it might as well have been a rainbow and unicorns.

The flight attendant felt tired all of a sudden. She lay down with thoughts of pretty boy from the coffee shop in her head.

3

THE BARISTA, better known as Purple Hair, struggled to wake up. She felt as if someone was sitting on her chest, crushing the bones there, compressing her lungs. She tried to tell herself it was just that thing that happened to her sometimes, that feeling of trying to wake up but being unable to move. Sleep paralysis? Yeah, that had to be it.

Screaming.

She was screaming.

It sounded like her voice was coming from under water, low and muffled. Frantic.

Quiet... no. Silent.

Could anyone hear her?

She thought she was hyperventilating, thought she was using her full voice to scream for release, but she wasn't so sure. Was she moving? In her mind she was, arms flailing, hands grasping for purchase. But was she?

She raised her hand in front of her face—sent that very signal to her mind and willed her hand to rise, but it didn't. It didn't and she wasn't screaming, wasn't moving, wasn't hyperventilating. Was she breathing at all?

There was something at the foot of her bed.

Dark and shadowy, floating above her feet, its toes aligned with her own, one cracked and yellowed claw reaching toward her chipped manicured big toe.

Shit.

She blinked—it was still there.

She tried to move her toe away, but she couldn't—she didn't even flinch.

She screamed louder still, begging the thing over her bed, the thing clad in black rags that billowed around its form and was carried on an unseen wind—the thing that was lifting its head to look at her ever so slowly—to leave her alone. She cried, her voice cracking, her sanity fracturing.

And then it was gone, and she was screaming her most blood-curdling horror movie scream aloud in her bedroom, the sound reverberating off the walls like she was in an echo chamber. Soon her mother would rush into her room, terrified by what she might find after a scream like that, but for now she was alone, lying in her bed staring at her foot, the chipped manicure seeming to glow from her big toe.

Her chest heaved.

A sheen of sweat cooled in the morning air.

Her throat was raw before she finished. When her finger twitched beside her, fluttering against her leg gently, much like the touch of eyelashes in a discreet butterfly kiss, her heart nearly stopped.

The book lay open on her nightstand, marking the page she had started to read but had fallen asleep on. When had she placed the book there? She could remember falling asleep on it, the book slipping out of her hands and landing… where? The floor? The bed? Her legs? She didn't know. But there it was, waiting for her to pick it up, to read it; to finish what she started.

She wanted to get up, wanted to splash water on her face,

maybe go downstairs and talk with her mother, ask her about her day. Funny how that's what she was thinking about right then—talking with her mom. She hadn't been interested in just having a conversation with her in a long time—longer than she could remember. She didn't think about that normally—didn't think about her mother at all, really. She was 19—it was normal. That's what her mother told her, even as her eyes showed the sadness that her voice denied. She hadn't thought about doing it, just sitting with her mom and talking maybe over a cup of coffee, the way they used to, before school and work and boyfriends and parties had taken over her life, but it was all she wanted to do right then. She sat up, intent on doing just that, swinging her legs off the bed with less effort than she expected and moving to stand… but she couldn't. She couldn't roll herself off the bed either as she attempted next, her panicked mind telling her she'd better get off the bed or she would die there.

She was stuck.

She didn't know if the book floated in the air, moving of its own volition, to rest in her open hands, but somehow it was there. The words on the page seemed emblazoned in gold.

Pretty.

As her mind begged her to shut her eyes, to throw the book across the room, to get up and burn it where it landed, she read the title of the new story, her eyes tracing the words as if they were sacred. With a sigh that was both fearful and expectant, she settled into the tale, her purple hair falling into her eyes as she read.

The Garage Door

There's something to be said about the stamina of a 4-year-old. People are always saying, 'I wish I could bottle some of that energy,' or some other annoying little comment that always strikes me as hollow. Those cute little one-offs always made people sound like they are just trying to find something nice to say to draw attention from the fact that the kid in question is acting like he's hopped up on something. The 'I've been where you are' comment that older ladies say to young mothers when their children run wild in the aisles of department stores, or when they eat all of the grapes before they are paid for, or, and this is priceless, when Junior decides it's time for American Idol *tryouts at the deli counter, is really judgment thinly-veiled as commiseration. 'Tsk tsk,' that seemingly understanding smile really says. Get your shit together, Miss. But of all the offhanded comments made by spectators of the parental variety show, that one rings true. Now, as the mother of three, shall we say, spirited children, I do want to bottle that energy. I'd sell it to folks in their fifties who are just starting to realize that the flexibility from their youth is never coming back. I'd sell it to people trying to lose weight; jumping around like the Energizer bunny from sunup to sundown will surely do the trick. I'd sell it to anyone who wanted it and make a mint. Even at $1 a bottle, I'd be a millionaire within days. But one of life's cruel jokes is that you can't bottle it. You can't put it in the freezer to defrost when you really need it. All you can do it use it when you have it.*

My 4-year-old understands that concept really well.

I thought maybe we could watch a little TV after music class and a play date at the park. Thought just maybe we could relax a little before naptime when I would, inevitably, fall asleep too, missing my chance to get something done. There's only a short window between having one wild thing in the house and three—just about an hour and a half. I try to vacuum, do some laundry, clean up, start dinner, and sit down for 10 minutes in that time. Sometimes I can get one or two things on the list done, but on days like today, when Mr. Baby is excited about everything he sees, I don't do anything but sleep. So I sigh, as my eyes get heavy, and settle in to a nice recline on the couch, watching Nick wind down like a top losing its juice. I didn't realize I was lying down until he climbed on top of me and got comfortable, his head on my chest, his soft hair tickling my nose. Maybe we'll just stay here on the couch for our nap instead of trudging upstairs to the bedroom. The TV's on but that's ok. It's on a kiddie channel, so there's no chance of us waking up to a mob movie or something like that. As Nick put his arms around me, his clammy skin sticking to mine, feeling good in a way that only moms know, I decided that yeah, a nap on the sofa with my little guy would be perfect.

The sound of the garage door opening should have woken me up, but it didn't.

Oh, I heard it (its low hum is unmistakable through our paper-thin walls), but I didn't wake up. I should have—the door opening in the middle of the day is unusual to say the least. My other two kids don't get out of school for hours and Chris isn't due home from work until after six. More disturbing is the fact that knowing these things, I still didn't get up. Someone could be breaking in. Or what if we overslept and the kids were opening the door with the keypad? What if someone was making them open the door with the keypad? For some reason, in that place between deep sleep and awake, I didn't think either of those things was happening. I just figured it was Chris. He was home early, and that was all it was. Some part of my subconscious wondered why he was home early—slow day at work; playing hooky; laid off?—but didn't care enough to wake my body up to find out.

At first.

Chris took a long time getting into the house. In fact, I never heard him come inside, but I heard him moving around. That was weird because I could hear Nick's rhythmic breathing, could feel his hair under my nose if I reached for the sensation like a swimmer coasting to the surface for a breath of fresh air. But the door didn't unlock, and the alarm didn't announce his arrival with a beep. He was just there all of a sudden, puttering around in the room. I heard him drop a bag, then unzip it and rummage around inside. I heard the volume on the television turn up—one of those incessant cartoon jingles blaring suddenly; ramming the sugary-sweet lyrics about a being four and, each day, growing some more down my ear canal, as if I couldn't already recite them in my sleep. I heard footsteps, Chris' socked feet approaching Nick and I on the sofa to kiss our heads like he always does when he finds us asleep on lazy weekends. I could feel myself straining towards his lips, expectantly reaching for his touch. But none came. Instead I heard raspy breathing overlaying a sickening whine—barely audible, but there, persistently there. It was so primal it affected my soul. I felt the heat from his skin as he stood over me, leaning in to peer into my face. I heard him lick his lips, his tongue flicking out like a snake's over dry lips.

That was enough to get my attention.

It wasn't that I hadn't heard ragged breath from Chris before. It had been a while, but not that long. Something about this sound, the base desperation in it, made me feel different. The usual butterflies in my stomach followed closely by warmth cascading down past my navel didn't happen. Instead I felt a sensation that I couldn't really put a finger on. Edginess? Maybe. Fear? I didn't want to admit that.

I tried to open my eyes, ready to tell him about the weirdness that started the moment he came home. He would appreciate it for what it was—an overactive imagination going full tilt. I felt. It was obviously because of Nick's clammy skin and the drool that had slipped out of his mouth and onto my skin. That's why I was thinking about a wolf or a dog that we don't have, or some other panting, heavy breathing thing. He would laugh and hug me the way I like and everything would be fine. If I'm lucky, maybe I can slip out from under Nick without waking him and have a little play date of my own. But I couldn't get my eyes to obey me. They were stuck together so well, it was as if they had been glued. I couldn't stop my mind from going to a place I had hoped I would forget. When in the dim room blanketed by humidity so stifling it was tangible, and surrounded by the sickeningly sweet-smelling combination of fresh flowers and cheap perfume, I must have been the only one to see the glue giving way on Uncle Wally's eyes, the whites (well, grays considering his state of repose) winking out at me. But this time my memory of that day distorted into something far worse. Uncle Wally's right eye opened all the way, blinked, and then he turned his head toward me, his neck popping and cracking as he did it.

I tried to scream. I knew I would scare Nick and ruin any chance of having a little afternoon happy, but I needed to wake up and in a hurry. Before Uncle Wally decided to get out of the coffin and come see me. But I couldn't. I felt like my mouth was open, but there was no sound coming from my stretched vocal cords. I tried to sit up, to shake myself out of this crazy vision (oh God, why is Uncle Wally smiling?) but I couldn't move. I started to panic. I could still hear that feral breathing over me, like an animal waiting for the right time to pounce. I could see Uncle Wally lifting his head out of the coffin, his body slow to react, but moving, nonetheless. I imagined that Nick, my sweet little boy, was staring at me as I struggled, his face unreadable, impassive... cold.

I screamed.

I screamed long and loud. But that's not what I heard. The smallest, weakest crescendo emitted from my lips, building to a faint whimper, before all my limbs jumped to attention at one time. The jerk snapped me out of whatever spell I was under. It also woke Nick, my beautiful, still asleep and not staring at his mom like she was an experiment boy, up.

"Mommy! No!" He protested groggily. I kissed him on his head, the action making me acutely aware of the fact that we were alone in the room and laid him down on the sofa. Children have an uncanny ability to fall back to sleep right away as though nothing happened. I was grateful for that today.

The room was still. I don't know why, but that made me uneasy. I mean, it should have been still if there were really only

Nick and I at home, but just seconds before, I knew someone was in the room with me. Knew, not felt. And now there was no one here.

Was this a game? I almost let myself buy into that as I stood tentatively and peered into the kitchen. Hide and seek maybe? Come find me, and quick so we can steal a couple of minutes to ourselves? I wanted to believe that. But as I saw the red Virginia clay on the floor leading from the family room—from the very sofa Nick and I were on—to the garage, I knew it wasn't true.

I thought I had shut my eyes. I imagined I was standing in the family room, facing the dining room, imagined I was still waiting for Chris to pop out and whisk me to the bedroom. It was safer than where I ended up. But the door handle beneath my outstretched hand couldn't be ignored. Neither could the hot air that hit me in the face like a blast from an oven when I opened the door. I tried to shut my eyes then, tried to will away the sight of it all. But I couldn't. Partly because it didn't make sense. Chris' car would have been in the place where his shoe lay on its side. It would have filled the space where his leg bent obscenely under his body if he had come home. But he didn't come home, did he? He was still at work.

Chris' eyes were cloudy, his beautiful brown covered in a white film. That doesn't happen right away, the part of my mind that was fighting off the paralysis that fear was trying to impose, rationalized. It takes at least a couple of hours for that to happen, right?

I stood there trying to figure out what I was looking at, my mind flitting back and forth between thinking it was an elaborate dream or if I was standing on some alternative plane, where reality was just a little different than the one I am from. I was in the zone; sweat coating my brow as I tried to make sense of the scene playing out in my garage, when the shuffling of feet brought me back to reality. And Chris was still there.

"Mommy, I don't wanna be 'wake," Nick said rubbing his eyes, the beginnings of a major pout sprouting on his lips. I looked at him, his hair all over his head, his eyes squinted against the light, and then back into the garage at the man I planned to spend the *rest of my life with, and bit my lip. I wanted to keep biting and biting until I drew blood. Maybe that would snap me out of it. Maybe the dead Chris would disappear.*

I didn't want Nick to see anything, so I closed the garage door. With any luck I could keep him away from the garage until everything was said and done and Chris had been moved.

Uncle Wally's joyless smile nagged at me.

I bit my lip a little harder than usual (just in case) and let the sob that was rushing from my throat turn into a yawn.

"Me either, baby. Me either."

"Honey?"

Leslie was so tired of yelling. She yelled up the stairs, yelled through doors, yelled into other rooms because her lovely daughter always had headphones, earbuds, AirPods—whatever they were called—jammed into her ears, blocking out all other sound She was always in another world... a world Leslie wasn't sure how to navigate anymore.

She needed to go. The longer she waited to get on the road, the longer it would take to get there. Traffic was horrendous these days—one of the only things that hadn't changed in the past few years... her commute sucked then, and it sucked now. Normally she would have just left, but she really needed her daughter to answer her, to acknowledge her request this time. She needed her to take the dog to the vet on her way to work. Leslie couldn't do it herself—it was too early. She had written a note, but Leslie wasn't sure that was enough.

"Ok?" Leslie tried again, "I can't take her, and she has to go today. If you leave her there, I will pick her up on my way back home, ok?"

Nothing.

Not a peep.

Damn it, Leslie thought. *This girl is going to make me climb the stairs and look her in the eyes.*

Leslie went upstairs again and knocked on her daughter's bedroom door.

"Babe?"

No reply.

She turned the knob and pushed the door open. She couldn't help the smile that spread on her face as she spied her daughter's purple hair splayed on the pillow. Purple hair, she snickered as she walked toward the bed. If she's not careful, she'll burn all the ...hair... out of her...

Leslie's mind almost didn't process what her eyes were seeing. There was too much red where there shouldn't have been, too much all over her chest, all over the bedsheets, all over. Her nose had bled, that's all, right? It was just a nosebleed; Leslie could see the stream as it trailed from her nostrils. So, why didn't she just get up? Why didn't she just wipe her nose and get up from that dirty bed and change her clothes?

Leslie couldn't move, couldn't breathe... couldn't think.

She never heard herself wailing, never saw herself clawing at her daughter, yanking at her arms, shaking her shoulders, begging her to wake up. Leslie never saw the book that she tripped over, the one that sent her careening into her daughter's headboard, splitting her own skin and letting blood to mingle with her child's. She only felt the purple hair beneath her fingers, purple hair made brittle from so many dye treatments, purple hair that would fade underground, where no one would see.

4

SHE HATED GOING to those things.

Picking through someone's garbage, like a homeless person looking through trash cans for scraps.

So what you could get good deals?

So what people let go of perfectly good stuff—unopened stuff—that you might never have bought new yourself.

So what?

Yard sales were not the way she wanted to spend her Saturday mornings, but also, so what? This is what the senior center director told her to do. That and teach the old girls how to make jewelry—beaded rings, bracelets, and necklaces to accessorize their brightly colored outfits from Chico's.

It was hot out. She could make a case for them cutting their yard sale hopping short because of it.

Jenn got out of the van—the standard issue senior center go-mobile—and called to one of the women in her little group outing.

"Carol..." Jenn tried but realized mid-yell that the poor dear wouldn't hear her; her hearing aid was a bright fuchsia that seemed to glow against her silver hair and was definitely out of range.

Jenn started to approach Carol, feeling like she might melt in the early morning heat, but doubled back to the van to grab the ladies some water. Surely they were feeling it too. With five bottles in hand, condensation sweating off of them immediately and wetting her pants, Jenn started out again, this time seeing Samantha nearby as Carol had moved on to another table. Samantha, her southern belle, the leader of the crew, the one who called the shots. She was holding a book gingerly, rotating it in her hands, running her fingers over the gilded lettering.

"Samantha… you thirsty?"

Jenn held out the water to the woman who didn't pay her a second glance. She had shrunk as old people often do, standing about shoulder height to Jenn's 5'5" frame, but anyone who saw that and assumed her diminutive stature equaled weakness had another thing coming. Samantha was cunning and sharp, ready with a response that would cut you down and make you want to sit in a corner for a while. She had heard Jenn perfectly. There was nothing wrong with her hearing unlike many of the others. She just deigned not to respond.

Jenn smirked. It was too hot for this shit.

She retracted the arm holding the water like a good little girl and stepped closer to look at the ornate cover.

"Whatcha got there?"

"A book, dear," Samantha said, condescension lacing her words.

"I know *that*, but…" Jenn's eyes cascaded over the cover, swirls of gold atop hues of cinnamon and nutmeg. "What kind of book?"

Samantha looked up at the girl. She was a nice enough sort, unremarkable, but that was ok. She did her job well enough and stayed out of everyone's hair, her nose stuck in her phone when her tasks were done. She let them alone, and that was precisely how Samantha liked it. At least she didn't have to battle with her tooth and nail over everything like she had the last one. Samantha snorted quietly at the thought.

Samantha handed her the book and pointed at the title. "*The Tales of Time*," Samantha read aloud, almost irreverently, like she was holding some cherished tome from before her time. Truth was, she had never heard of the book, and reading had been her favorite pastime for most of her 83 years. She had been ready to crack the book open, to turn the yellowed pages and find out what the story was about, but she opted instead to let the girl do it. Infusing a little awe in her voice for the hell of it, she continued, "I've never seen one quite like this before."

It was true. She hadn't seen one quite like that before. She hadn't *ever* seen a book so beautiful and delicate like that one before.

Samantha looked at the girl with wide eyes for little added drama—the icing on the cake—before shuffling down the table to look at other things. She laughed under her breath as she saw the girl turn the book over in her hands, water bottles forgotten on the edge of a table crowded with baby clothing and toys. *Maybe she'll buy it, read something she can hold her in her hand for a change*, Samantha thought. These kids and their smartphones—no wonder everyone's eyes were going bad. She adjusted her glasses on the bridge of her nose. It had taken her until age 70 to need to wear them all the time, even with all the reading she did. She was proud of that fact. At the rate most young people were going, they'd be wearing glasses before they even turned 40.

Jenn ghosted her hand over the cover of the book, her fingers tensed in anticipation. In a distant corner of her mind, she was aware of how strangely she was behaving. She had never cared much for books, never read for fun at all, really. It was always part of a requirement for school or work. But for some reason, this book intrigued her. The look of it, the feel—soft in a velvety kind of way. She felt compelled to open it, like she really had to do it... Like she really had no choice at all.

She opened the book. Flipped past all of the blank pages until she found words. She settled herself to read as the sweat slid from the nape of her neck and down her spine.

The notification on her phone dinged so loudly, Jenn's knee jerked, slamming into the table, knocking over the bottles of water she had brought for the ladies and some of the baby clothes too.

"Oh dear," Samantha fussed, coming back to the flustered girl's side, bending to pick up the water bottles before Jenn snapped out of her surprise and stopped her.

"Don't Samantha; I've got it. You round the girls up and let's get out of here. It's hotter than Hades out here."

Samantha made agreeable *mmhmming* sounds as she walked towards her friends, more tickled than she should have been about the scene that had played out before her. *It's the little things,* she had always said, and that mantra still rang true.

Sun-ho posted a video.

That's what the message said.

Jenn couldn't help the smile that crossed her face as she penciled in time to watch it later, once she got the girls situated back at the center. She couldn't wait to see if he was going to talk about his upcoming concert. Maybe he would sing for them a little or show them a dance routine that would be in the show...

The book felt substantial in her hand.

"Excuse me," she called out after picking up the baby

clothes and folding them in a way that hid the dirt she had put there when knocking them to the ground, "how much for this book?"

Idol

"How can he be that beautiful?"

Millie stared in awe at the image on her smartphone, enlarging his lips, his eyes, even his undercut for a closer look. The sigh that escaped her lips was heavy with sweet admiration and laced with feels she hadn't been aware of before finding K-Pop. It didn't take long for her to become entrenched in the mania. She found her favorite group almost right away, their luxurious voices caressing lyrics she didn't understand, creating an exotic, taboo-like aura in her room when she put on their songs... which was every day, for most of the day. She bought all the stuff: the summer video packages, the CDs with special photo albums inside, the swag featuring her bias and the one showcasing her bias wrecker (then, guiltily, something with the faces of the other members too because how could she truly be a fan if she only supported a few of the members, right?). Millie had it all. They were going to be performing in the US later that year and Millie had a great idea to pitch to her mom about travelling to LA to see them. LA is a lot closer than South Korea, she would say. I can work during the summer to help out on costs, she would add. Maybe her mom would understand. She'd had her own entertainer crush, right? I mean, what were all those tears about when Prince died if she didn't? Millie thought she probably shouldn't go there, not unless she really had to. Mom hasn't listened to Prince since he died—the mourning was real.

His oval eyes looked out at her from behind a fan of periwinkle-colored bangs (oh, how her bias loved to change his hair color!), giving all the fanservice he knew she and the millions of other screaming teenage girls around the world liked. He had just woken up in some other place on the other side of the world from where she sat and decided to go live on YouTube just because. Millie grinned from ear to ear when she got the notification and left the dinner table without warning. Her father said, "Don't forget about the movie," or something like that as she passed by him. Millie had shoved earbuds in her ears before taking her plate to the sink and had turned the volume up high so that she could hear every nuance of his voice before reaching the stairs.

She thought she grunted a response to her father but wasn't sure.

His face was filling her screen before she had gotten out of the room; his perfect pink lips parted suggestively as he worked to get the camera situated just right. She never saw her brother Chris smirking at her from the kitchen as she raced by, never saw her cat dodging her legs as they scissored wildly up the stairs. She only saw him, only heard his groggy voice speaking in his hypnotic foreign tongue.

He yawned.
Millie smiled.
He chuckled.
Millie blushed.

"MILLIE HASN'T COME DOWN YET?" her mother asked of no one in particular. The kitchen was clean, and the leftovers put away. It was time for movie night, and three of the four of their little family were ready to get started.

Chris looked up, shrugged, and turned his attention back to the game he was playing on his smartphone. Millie's father sighed and said, "No, not yet."

Millie's mom looked up at the ceiling, a move she swore helped her to hear what was going on upstairs better, and listened intently. The muffled sound of a male voice speaking quickly could be heard. She didn't notice the staticky hiss that was deliberately, persistently there, but inconspicuously so. Like the assumption of crackling on the wind after an electric shock, the sound floated among the waves and pitch to mingle with his rich baritone. She strained, trying to understand something of what was being said, trying to determine whether the broadcast was almost over or not. She wanted to give her daughter a chance to join the family activity on her own. Choosing her battles these days, Millie's mom didn't relish the idea of pulling her away from something she wanted to do. On any given day, Millie might as easily bite her head off as give her a smile, and if the guy that was talking was the one from that K-Pop group she liked, and Millie tried to interrupt her...

"Go get your sister," their mom said to Chris reluctantly.

Chris' nose was stuck in the game. He was oblivious.

She looked at Chris and then over at her husband incredulously.

He cleared his throat first but got no reaction.

"Chris!" His voice boomed in the room.

Chris looked up, surprised.

"Your mother told you to go and get your sister."

The protest that rose in Chris' throat died on his lips when he saw the frustration in his father's eyes. He got up without a word, leaving his phone behind as he knew they wanted him to. Chris didn't want to fight. He wanted to watch the movie. This week had been his choice, and he couldn't wait to rub it in Millie's face. He had chosen Child's Play, mostly because he knew Millie hated Chuckie. Crazy little demon doll, here we come.

Chris bounded up the stairs, talking all the way. "Time to say goodnight, sweetheart," he parodied, trying to sound lovey-dovey. "It's time for the movie." He stopped outside her door, hearing a male voice speaking in a language he didn't understand. "You don't even know what he's saying, Mil." Chris turned the knob and opened her door, still talking. "He could be telling you to take off your clothes in front of class and do the dance from his last video." This struck Chris as incredibly funny.

Chris' hearty laughter turned shrill, like the scream of a siren, when his sister turned toward him slowly. It wasn't the saliva that spilled from the corners of her mouth that frightened him most, nor the milky white veil that covered her chestnut brown irises. It was the way she spoke that sent chills down his spine; the monotone delivery of a question he could not understand,

"Eotteohge geuleohge aleumdab ji?"

5

THEY DIDN'T TELL them much about what happened to that poor girl—really only said that she died as a result of natural causes, some kind of brain aneurysm or some such thing. But Samantha knew better. Even when the women who took her jewelry class said they thought something was off about her that last week, thought maybe she wasn't feeling her best (they said she looked a bit peaked in class, especially when she was trying to thread the clear beads for the crochet rope bracelet she was planning to teach them to make that day)—even then, Samantha didn't buy it. She tried to tell Clarise about it, tried to remind her that aneurysms didn't show themselves like that. Jenn wasn't sick, wasn't tired, wasn't anything. She just up and died, and none of the people who saw her making bracelets or serving juice or tapping her foot in the back of the room during country line dance class saw it coming.

Samantha hadn't gotten to be 83 years old being stupid. She knew better than to believe what the staff told her about Jenn. Whatever happened to Jenn wasn't natural at all.

Samantha saw the book among Jenn's things as she was

leaving the center for what would be the last time. It was sitting there, propped on its side in a box alongside a coat, a picture of the girl with an older man, and all the knickknacks that seem to follow people from desk to desk, job to job. She reached towards it, wanting to touch the cover, lured by that gorgeous gilding work she had so admired that day at the yard sale. How intricate it was, how detailed. Such crafts-manship didn't exist anymore, it seemed. Samantha hadn't realized how much she missed it. It was like art inasmuch as the words themselves were and the creation of beautiful things seemed to be in short supply. She had woken up with that very notion in her mind that day, the fragment of a poem on the air that swirled between sleep and consciousness,

My darling, what speak you,
a voice
his voice
yet not
asked thunderously,
for I have not gone

Lyrical words. Pretty words chaperoning her from sleep from a poem she couldn't place—at least not yet. She wanted to think about it more, maybe search for it online as they say —put technology to good use. Thoughts of white horses on a backdrop of the blackest of nights filled her head.

"It's beautiful, isn't it?"

The voice, belonging to the prune-faced lady that sat at the front desk, surprised her. It wasn't only that she was speaking in a kind voice that Samantha had never heard from her before in all the time she had been going to the center that threw her for a loop. It was that she was speaking at all. That woman, whose name Samantha had never both-ered learning, seemed to prefer frowning to smiling as she sat in the air-conditioned front office, the same papers scattered on her desk from one day to the next. That she nodded her head hello and goodbye was the only indication any of them had that she was still alive.

"That it is," Samantha responded belatedly. The woman had moved behind the desk upon which the box sat, standing opposite Samantha expectantly. What was she looking at? Samantha found herself more irritated than she expected to be at being observed.

Where the hell was the shuttle?

She decided to grab it, to pick the book up and feel it before old prune face moved the box away.

"These are Jenn's belongings…," the woman started.

"I was with her when she found it," Samantha countered, feeling the lie forming on her tongue. "I am so glad I saw this —I didn't want to have to contact the family for it."

"Contact the family? For what?"

"This book," Samantha continued settling into the story. "I bought it for her, well not really *for* her… but I let her read it first. When she was done she was going to give it back to me, but now…" She ran her hand over the velvety cover and had to suppress an appreciative moan.

"Oh," Prune Face said, unsure what to do.

"I guess I might as well just take it with me tonight," Samantha said, tucking the book under her arm and taking a step toward the door, silently hoping the shuttle would pull up and whisk her away with her stolen goods. "Doesn't make sense to do much else."

The woman nodded with Samantha, going along with whatever she wanted. Everyone knew Samantha, knew how she was… it was easier that way. Samantha continued to shuffle toward the door, decision made, will imposed. The woman sat down behind the desk and watched her go.

6

THEY MET every week but it hadn't gotten any easier. Not for Karli. Not for Kevin either if the way he always leaned on the wall, backing himself into a corner so that he couldn't be surprised by someone coming up behind him, tapping his shoulder, singling him out was any indication. He never volunteered, always remained in the shadows, made himself as small as he could with his almost 6'0" tall frame. She'd talked with him once when they were on a break, everyone immediately crowding the snack table hoping that the food would chase away the jitters, and he told her it was his nerves that kept him quiet. Karli had responded with something nice enough, something people said when someone they didn't know well seemed to be teetering on the edge of sharing too much, something like, 'Yeah, we're all pretty nervous' or 'the struggle is real' – non-committal, perfunctory, placating. He nodded and fell silent again, filling his plate with the lukewarm cheese and stale crackers that had been left out since they filed into the space, a backroom at a rec center that had seen better days. Karli remembered when the rec center had a preschool in it, a Tae Kwon Do class, senior citizen dances, and, of course, the requisite Bingo. But none of that happened anymore. Now the activities were comprised of AA meetings and support groups, self-help seminars from people who had gotten on, fallen off, and gotten back on a myriad of wagons. Instead of smiling faces glistening with sweat, high on endorphins or sugar, determination etched lines in the countenances of the people who exited those doors now. And then there was the ragtag group she was involved in, many of whom looked like they had wandered into the wrong room.

The fluorescent light in the hallway flickered. It always did. One day it was going to go out, and they'd be stuck back there, in a forgotten room off a dark hallway.

Karli wondered if she could write something about that.

The quiet man floated away, gliding as if he were carried by the wind, not making a sound as he moved – barely shifting the air at all, as if he were never there to begin with. He settled back into his corner then much like he had that day; the only difference was that now there was a sizeable printout from Ms. Watson in his hands. She had spent some bucks on that thing: she had made copies for each one of them – 12 in all. Karli was lost in thought about how she must have gotten hold of the copier at work and run them off because she couldn't see the woman who brought them stale crackers every meeting actually paying for copies. Karli thought about how the crackers really were stale every single time, how she must have dug into the back of her pantry to find ones that were out of date and taking up space to give them. She wondered how much Ms. Watson got paid to run the workshop, wondered if it had a stipend in it for snacks, because if it did, she was definitely not using it on them. And the light in the hallway kept flickering.

Ms. Watson said she used to worked mostly off-off-Broadway, but unless "off-off" meant outside of New York,

she was full of shit. The lady who ran the Nicotine Anonymous group said she remembered seeing her in a show
somewhere in Virginia back when those were her stomping
grounds. She said she was pretty good if you liked the melodramatic type. Karli laughed and asked her if there was any
other kind of actress which earned her a smile from a mouth
not used to contorting in that way. Still Karli enjoyed the
class for what it was worth, which was about $25 a month at
present. She went every week, projected her voice, and tried
to 'find her presence'. Whatever. It was a way to spend a few
hours. So if the heavyset lady who looked less like an actress
and more like a schoolteacher who should have retired five
years before wanted to make up stories about having been on
the big stage, so be it. Karli didn't have the energy to call her
on it.

Once everyone settled – she always waited for people to
quiet down before she moved to the center of the room to
speak, commanding an audience at all times – Ms. Watson
made her way to the middle of the makeshift circle they had
constructed to mimic a stage using rickety chairs, desks, and
empty garbage cans to affect the look. She took a deep
breath as she looked around the room, and then another, her
way of urging everyone to follow suit. And they played
along – there wasn't anything else to do other than that.
After her third breath where she almost swooned as she let
her eyes flutter closed and her chest heave with the effort,
she began.

"OK. Today is going to be special. Today… we are going…
to act!"

She swung her arms in grand fashion to indicate that
acting was this massive undertaking that we, her lowly
students, were now ready to embark upon. It was grand –
like Yul Brynner in *The King and I* grand, big and bold and
loud and gaudy. Theatrical at its most melodramatic, and it

was then that Karli knew that every single thing the nicotine lady had said about Ms. Watson was true.

"Today *you* will take center stage. You will stand where I am standing right now and deliver emotion like you never have before. This goes beyond delivering lines. It's passion that I'm looking for here. You should be able to make us cry, laugh, feel pleasure and pain just by the look on your face, your posture, your body language."

She punctuated her words by moving her short arms through a series of pushes and pulls, stretches designed to look fluid and graceful but most decidedly did not. But she believed in whatever she was doing completely; in her mind her display, her garish gesticulations were as poignant a those seen in the best of performances - *Les Misérables* at the Barbican or *A Raisin in the Sun* at the Barrymore. Karli sniffed her inner stage snob – the one from another life where she collected playbills in shadowboxes that lined her walls and recited lines to imaginary castmates… the one she would never admit to – back inside herself, forced it to quiet down and go back into its cubby.

"You hold your performance piece in your hand," Ms. Watson continued, thumbing the side of the packet. "All you need to do is pick the one that speaks to you most."

People started to look at the papers in their hands like they were a new type of animal, unnamed and wild. They looked at the packet in reverent silence and something about that made the hair on the back on Karli's neck stand on end. It also caused a tickle to form in her throat… a tickle that would turn into full-fledged laughter if she wasn't careful. She watched them, this timid bunch of misfits that came together to find some way to spend their time other than on the streets with a bottle in their hands or a dime bag in the pants, awed by the experiment in human nature she was witnessing. Some braved their consternation enough to raise the cover a little, just enough to peek inside. Most just stared at the blank cover, caught in a strange limbo.

The girl with oily hair and a dirty nose ring spoke first.

"These are just a bunch of stories," she said, her voice thick with mucus before she sniffed it back into her nose. "How are we supposed to act something out if there are no lines to say at all?"

"As I said, Mara," Ms. Watson said exasperatedly, and Karli started to wonder if she was right about that name or if she had just pulled it out of the air, "the lines themselves are less important than the emotions you act out. Draw us in with your body language. Did you know that there is a Danish actor who can make you feel five different emotions in the span of fifteen seconds, all without moving his body at all? It's all in his eyes, his facial expressions," she looked away at nothing the way that theater folk often do, the look on her face nothing short of rapturous. "It's absolutely brilliant."

Ms. Watson turned her attention back to the group with obvious effort and looked each of them in the eye.

"Do that. These stories are all in first person. Do you remember what that means...?" Crickets.

"Neil?"

Neil should have cleared his throat before he started speaking; the gravelling, phlegmy thing that came out made Karli want to gag.

"Um, yeah, it's like when you use I and me," he said, the unspoken question raising his voice a few octaves indication that he wasn't at all sure that he was right.

"That's exactly right. They are all told from the character's perspective. You need to *become* the character. Make us feel what *you* feel. If your character cries in the story, then you should cry too. If you want to be great, you have to master this."

Pause. Indeed, a *dramatic* pause during which the class

looked back at her with vacant eyes. They didn't want to be great, their expressions should have told her. They just wanted to exist. If she saw the messages written on most of their faces, she ignored them.

"Ok! So, go find a seat and read the material in the packet and-"

"All of it?" an older Latinx man said, the irritation at the prospect of having to go through all of the stories in that twenty-page packet written on his face.

"If you want to pick a story that you can embody, one that speaks to you and only you, yes. If you don't care, well," she shrugged one shoulder in that aloof way that dismissed the intended recipient and cast a cold pall over the others in close proximity, "I guess that will show in your performance, won't it?"

He sighed and so did someone else sitting behind Karli but she didn't turn around to see who it was. She was too busy looking at the light in the hallway, the way it flickered on then off, on... off...

Maybe she'd write something about that sooner rather than later.

"I would urge you to look at all of the stories. If you pick one of the stories in the beginning of the book simply because you want to be done with the assignment, you might miss a gem waiting for you at the back of the book."

Ms. Watson nodded at each of them, expecting reciprocation. Most acquiesced as people always do. Even Karli found herself nodding back in agreement even though she had no intention of reading the stories in the no-name, photocopied book, not when the light kept calling to her the way it did. If she couldn't finish writing the story before all the ones in the book were chosen, she would act out whichever one was left. How hard could it be?

"Ok, so let's get started," Ms. Watson finished. "With any

41

luck, you'll have selected your stories and we can have a few run-throughs tonight, before all is said and done."

Ms. Watson turned on her heel and went to the snack table. For a while her work was done, and she could indulge in the old cheese and crackers left to decompose in the stuffy, heavy air that always seemed to hang with them there in that backroom, no matter how they tried to ventilate the space. The misfits found places to sit and pour over the stories, the strain of the exercise showing in their furrowed eyebrows and tense shoulders before even starting the first story.

Karli dug out a pen from the bottom of her burlap bag, flipped the book over to the back, and started to write.

The light flickering down the hall blinked like a strobe light. I felt like I would get dizzy if I kept watching it, but I couldn't pull my eyes away. It was pretty. I want to touch the light to see if it was hot because maybe it is *hot and then*

… And then?

Stuck.

Karli got stuck in the first 5 minutes and couldn't see a way out, couldn't figure out her next steps. Why would she touch the light? Of course it was hot! She would burn herself and then what? She tried scrapping the whole thing and starting again, this time without the detour of touching the light. She got to the point where her character flicked the light switch on then off, but the fluorescent light kept up its own beat anyway, and got stuck again.

She bit the cap of her pen.

She crossed out whole sentences and tried to rewrite them but nothing came.

Damnit.

Karli guessed she would be acting out a story from the book after all.

She opened the book and read the first page.

I Have Nothing to Wear

How does this go?

What do you wear to something like this?

Choker, accentuating the neck? V-neck to show more skin? Tight dress, short dress, loose dress, long dress, no dress, maybe pants instead?

Do you wear a jacket, a vest, ruffles, lace?

My hand lands on a crushed velvet top with buttons and strappy things, none of which I remember. When did I buy this?

Sequins?

No.

Burnout? That paper-thin material that always seems like it will rip and show off the things it barely concealed in the first place?

Maybe that. Yes, maybe so.

Do we dance or is this one of those drinking and smoking parties? I wouldn't mind feeling a body next to mine, pressed up close, hot breath on my neck –

Yeah, I'd better make sure my neck is out instead of in so I can feel all the sensations I am supposed to feel.

So...

Flower or stripes? Polka dots? Midriff shirt and leather shorts?

Damn, it's been a long time since I went out.

But he called and he's hungry and I want.

Karli turned the page before finishing, not wanting to waste too much time on one that she knew she wouldn't pick. She had spent enough time trying to write her own story and came up empty; she didn't want to lose any more precious minutes.

Because there really was a story in there for her – suddenly she could feel it.

The Cleansing

The flames licked, danced, engulfed the wood eagerly like a hungry beast. She watched it flicker then build, climbing the walls like vines on the side of a house, undulating against the wall like lovers.

Next.

She

It turned my stomach.

That from within the cabin I could still smell the eclectic perfume, a mix of fried chicken, wet pennies, and Eau De Toilette that only she could make sweet, made me weak-kneed. The scent, long cleared by earth and element, filled my nostrils as my mind first commands, then pleads, "You don't recognize, you don't recognize, you don't, you can't...."

Out of Time

Blind, aimless movement, like a wave crashing onto the shore, rolling over and flattening the sand, removing all distinguishing marks: the hearts carved by fallen branches, the initials inside.

K. T.
+
L. M.
4 eva

Or at least until the tide came in and wiped it all away.
Wiped away.
Obliterated.
Razed.
Like Gomorrah and the Arc.
Starting over.
Starting again.

Hands pushed and grabbed. Legs pedaled, propelling men, women, and children toward the back of the store. The sweater she had been looking at seemed to disappear into thin air as if part of a magic trick - now you see it, now you don't - the garden variety activity provided for the very old and the very young at resorts when the parents go off to play. It had been ripped out of her hands by someone running by, face a blur. The tag came off in her hand, one of its corners puncturing her skin to draw blood. She thought to put the wound to her mouth and lick at it in that vampiric way that people did when they saw their own blood in the open air, self-ishly recalling it into their own bodies before anyone else could partake. She thought to do so, to taste the metallic notes, but as the next person to barrel through the racked space nearly bowled her over, taking that route instead of the tiled path that was mobbed with runners from the café at the front of the store, the customer service section, and the bathrooms, she thought better of it. If her hand was in her mouth and she took another hit she might knock her own teeth out. She might bite so deeply into her flesh that the soft lapping of her tongue wouldn't be enough to assuage the pain.

Running.

Everyone was running. Yet their feet made no sound.

Because of the siren.

The siren started up, crescendoing to its highest point within seconds, its tone even and persistent. It sounded like an old-time ambulance, deep and full, not shrill even though the hair on her arms and the back of her neck stood up, responding to it the same way it did to high-pitched noises. She had always thought the gooseflesh came because of the shrieking nature of it all: babies crying, nails scratching on a chalkboard, the undertone of a fire alarm – that shrill beeping that seems to ring in the room even after the alarm has been turned off: all of it was enough to set her teeth on edge.

But that wasn't it.

That wasn't all.

The siren was going off.

The one that most people living there had never heard before, including her.

The siren that meant it was over.

Everything they knew was unequivocally, irreconcilably over.

Because They were there.

She watched an old man fall to his knees a few rows over from her. He had been in the toddler clothing section, perhaps shopping for his grandson, the one he would never see again because he would never get out of that store. She saw him drop to his knees because the racks that had separated his body from view just seconds before had been pushed aside, toppled, fallen upon. And there were bodies. Arms and limbs tangled, twisted, bent under the weight of their own bodies. Still. She felt her mouth open, felt her jaw unhinge as her eyes fell upon some of the bodies stacked on top of each other: big, small, tiny.

Tiny.

And there was blood.

THEY were there.

She tried to take a step, to run with the rest of them, to succumb to the understanding, the stark reality the older man had already allowed, to move, but she could do nothing, nothing, nothing at all as she thought of her parents probably trying to get into the basement, to get into the tub, to hole up like it was a tornado. She could do nothing as she thought of her dogs running around her house, ears flattened to their heads to block out the sound, whimpers escaping their throats – could imagine them bouncing nervously as they peered through the sliding glass door into their familiar yard, though that space likely didn't look so familiar anymore. She thought of her colleagues running into the storage closet like she would have if she hadn't gone out to lunch, pressing their bodies into a space filled with things that could kill them if turned into projectiles, but having nowhere else to go. And it wouldn't matter.

Because this wasn't a hurricane; this wasn't a tornado, or a tsunami, or dust storm, or any other kind of storm. It was Them.

It was THEM.

And it was time.

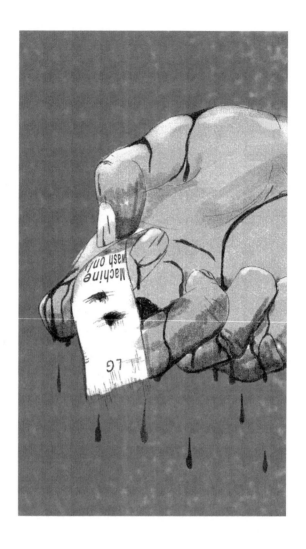

Awakening

Night when I thought it was day.

Cold, but unnaturally so, or so said the daffodils that had pushed through the ground already, showing their brilliant yellow. Unlike the pinks and reds and yellows of the azaleas that bloomed in my neighbor's yard, the ones she fussed over and pruned, the ones I vomited into over the fence before I fell... fell while we were talking about summer vacation and watching each other's dogs: fell and never got up again.

Days?

Weeks?

Years since that day, the world cycling on without a care while I lay in my grave, cold and dank, trying to get out.

To get out.

Because I shouldn't be there... I shouldn't be in the ground.

Locked away.

Forgotten.

Because I am here and I can remember the way the sun kissed his hair while we sat on the deck, how the night sky looked when it was full of stars.

Because I can remember what it was like to laugh and walk and run, yes run, so I did run because I could and my legs could still carry me. They carried me right back to where I should be. Right back home.

Cold.

Unseasonably cold for April or May or whatever month it was. Killing my daffodils. Killing my follower that would come up even if I wasn't there to see them.

So yellow. I want to touch one but I am afraid to ruin it. When I see my fingers in the moonlight, gnarled and discolored, bloody because I had been clawing, clawing, clawing at the lid of the grave, beating against the cement enclosure, kicking my way up through the dirt, dirt that fell into my eyes to blind me... dirt that slipped into my mouth and down my throat to choke. I was afraid to touch the daffodils, not because I didn't want to make them like me because they were already like me – dead and revived, awakened, denied rest. No, I didn't want to touch the daffodils because I would soil them with the dirt from my grave and the dirt was my own.

Happy.

Laughing.

Music in the night.

They were probably dancing, maybe watching a TV show, the kids might be playing a game and maybe cooking together in the kitchen, maybe...

A new car in the driveway.

A new car where mine used to be.

They were probably loving anew.

The wind guided my steps and for that I was thankful because it meant-

Close.

So many of the stories were close, but they whispered her name instead of screaming it, and she knew there was something else, something more just waiting for her to find it. Something inside her wondered why she cared, why all of a sudden, finding the right story was so important to her... why she was able to shut her eyes to what she saw happening around her: the cutter scratching at her scars, the alcoholic rubbing his mouth. That thing inside her wanted to ask if she was paying attention, if she had noticed that the guy who hung out in the shadows was suddenly not doing that anymore, that Kevin had, in fact, moved closer in to the group as if in search of kinship. It wanted to ask if she smelled the excitement coming off the middle-aged woman whose story Karli had not worked out yet. It wanted to ask her why she wasn't afraid. But it didn't. It stayed in the back of Karli's mind, circled in on itself, folding, tucking, receding... trying to disappear. Because Karli wasn't Karli anymore... not like she had been before opening that nameless book with stories copied off center on recycled paper. Karli wasn't who she needed to be to hear that part of herself anymore.

Because Karli was on the hunt. She wanted something she could sink her teeth into, something that had teeth of its own.

Another Day

It rained the day I took them, trapped them, kept them inside – clear, where I can see. I took them all, let them settle, mingle, comfort each other as they rippled, moved, fought against the confines, their pretty little place, until they stilled.

No, not all of them.

Some I sampled. I couldn't make myself wait, not knowing when the day would come when I could visit with them again. So I tried them – I tasted them. And I loved them.

I looked at them, those from that first day, that rainy day under a sky that seemed to hate me for what I was doing, sought to stop me by growling and clapping its hands. I looked at them every time I added another, even if I never looked at the other so often, never so intensely. I looked at them and they saw me too. They called my name and it made me smile.

Model Home

The light turned on in the darkness, a faint red glow indistinguishable in the unnatural greenish haze of night vision. Cabinets look creepy in the dark. So does the stillness of a sleeping house. Watching for too long can be terrifying – the feeling that something will show itself in the shadows is enough to drive someone mad.

Still, the camera came on for a reason...

Something floats before the lens. One would dismiss it as backscatter – indeed, most did that very thing – there is always dust in the air so the camera catching glimpses of it wouldn't surprise anyone except that shouldn't set off a motion sensored security camera. If a camera can be calibrated to ignore a 25-pound cat, then surely it should be able to discount a speck of dust. If they watched long enough they would see the orb take a decided turn and cross in front of the camera once more before travelling deeper in the room and disappearing into the shadows. Another speck of dust? Not likely.

But they wouldn't look that long – most people didn't. Because that's not what they would be looking for if they turned on this feed. There were countless other feeds of this very room when the demons came out to play, their forms sometimes translucent when wandering specters entered lost or angry; sometimes solid flesh and blood as looters lifted and squatters broke, but none of those recordings would be important if anyone found out about this one.

If they noticed.

It's there, just a little bit of heel, but still there, in view if you looked hard enough. But would they? Was anyone ever really looking anyway? It's late - past 3:30 a.m. Who would be looking at this hour anyway?

They wouldn't see in time, wouldn't be able to save him, this man whose heel is the only thing in the recording. A dark, solid colored sock – Black? Blue? - still covered the toes, but the heel was bare... brown skin against a backdrop of shadows in a darkened house in the middle of the night. Infrared will pick up something, make the heel more visible if nothing else, but what good would that do? From such a distance and without the benefit of the toes it won't look like much of anything – it could be a Styrofoam cup just as easily as the only thing visible of a dying man. And no one would think a Styrofoam cup suspicious, not with as many people that come in and out of this place every day. People were always in and out, picking up things, stealing things, chatting up the agent but never intending to buy. Sometimes the realtor invited her boyfriend over to have sex. Sometimes she hooked up with one of those people who had entered the house that day wandering, wandering, just like those wayward spirits. But the camera was never on then, so nobody ever knew. But it's on now – does it make a difference?

They brought him here to dump him, did away with the alarm before any notification could be sent, but not the camera sitting inconspicuously on the hutch, the one that had the broadest arc of the room. Different system – one of the really good ideas that the team designing the newer model homes came up with, because petty thieves wouldn't think outside of the box about a thing like that. As far as they were concerned, the place was empty at night which made it prime pickings. Snip, snip on the wires, use some computer geekery to screw up the Wi-Fi and you're in.

But these weren't thieves.

They brought him there to dump him, but he wasn't dead yet. They carried him in, left him there on the floor, and walked out, never realizing that he would squirm a little before he died, moving just enough to bring his heel into view, never realizing that he would add his low moans to the sounds of the house settling.

If the design team had thought about manning the camera, periodically watching live, they would have seen it. But they never would have saved him.

"Wh-where'd you get these stories? They're... there's...," someone started from the back of the room but Karli didn't look up from the book to see where the question came from. She didn't hear the answer either or if there even was one; she was engrossed in the next story in the book, each story getting closer and closer to the one that was written for her.

Even so, something in the back of Karli's mind reacted to the tone of the woman's voice and grew cold.

I Know

Shadows playing with the moon, making finger puppets on the wall and yes, I know that it's him and not me, that it's him come for me because he loves to play even if he has no hands to do it with anymore.

Cold.

Cold as the ice that encased him, trapped him, blanketed him below, down under, deep in the frigid blue. It's like that outside when the board creaks, and I feel it.

Beyond the Chain

I used to want to hear dogs barking, hear the laughter of children, get hit with the sprinkler every evening at dusk, and hope that baseballs didn't do any lasting damage. I wanted that, but what I got was a patch of grass hardly long enough for a grown man to lie down in heel-to-head, and trees so tall you could only see me in in the dead of winter, and then only if you squinted.

No dogs bark, no children play, not after they chained up the gate and took him away, not after what they found inside.

Gerald.

They never listened to him, not even when he swore he didn't know they were there, playing house in his shed, sitting around the table waiting for him to get home.

I knew they were there, but I couldn't tell.

I wouldn't tell.

They couldn't make me. Nothing could.

I knew they were they there, but they shouldn't have been. They were trespassing. They weren't invited. They didn't belong.

He said he didn't know, but that was a lie. He had to have known. I secretly think he put them there. For me. I fancied that for years, imagining that he had brought them there for me to see, for me to play with. I thought of what his voice might sound like when he told me to do what I wanted with them, that they were mine to do with what I would. He would sound strong and confident, nothing like the whimpering imbecile they dragged away that day, wide-eyed and pointing at me. I fantasized that he lied to them to make them stay, and oh, what a good liar he turned out to be! Maybe he told them that everything he did was for them, and that they had nothing to worry about because he cared for them and always would. Maybe he told them that my soul spoke to him and that I loved them too and that I wanted them there as much as he did. Their stench still sits in the wallpaper they had lined the walls of the shed with, trying to make the place look like a proper home.

He lied to himself about them, about me, about it all. Even as he set fire to the weeping willow that had been my friend, the massive thing that had sheltered cardinals and bluebirds over its 250-year life—even as he tried to use to it to burn away everything he ever knew, he couldn't murder the truth, couldn't clean away the stain. Even as he sits in his cell, far away from me now, still he knows, he remembers, he feels.

The table is still set for dinner, modestly, for three servings instead of five. The pitcher upon the table, with the painted rooster on the side and the chipped spout, is empty now, but that can be easily remedied. All one need do is ask.

No one comes past the chain or ventures into the woods to peek anymore—that time has long gone. Now they pass by without a second glance at the overgrown driveway, the cracked asphalt barely visible beneath layer upon layer of dead leaves and weedy undergrowth. Someone left candy once, had thrown it past the chain and into the gaping maw that yawned behind it.

Glasses

I went back for them.

I went back because I knew he dropped them and someone would see.

I saw them fly off his face and land in the mulch, one frame obliterated by the blast and the other cracked and splintered –

ruined beyond repair. They wouldn't need to be repaired, though; his blood smeared on the rim, on the lens, all over his face and hair, doubling back to mingle with what pooled in the gash at the top is his head told me so.

I went back for them.

I went back for them because I knew he'd want me too. I knew he'd like to have them with him wherever his body ended up, likely at the bottom of the quarry past the old farm because it was abandoned and the water was murky, filled with old shit that had sunk there decades ago — not even the sex-crazed idiots over at the high school used that spot for a romp because it was... there was just something off about it.

He'd like that.

If he had to die, he'd like to make a difference, and so I would put his body there. There he could be part of the lore, be one of the ghosts that haunted that old, shut down place.

Plus nobody would think to look there because nobody would have the guts to.

I went back for them, and they were there, right where he left them, right where they landed when they fell off after his eye was ruined and his face collapsed, little bones poking through the skin, piercing, cutting, flaying.

Except they were different.

They were bloodless.

The temples — arms, I called them, but he knew what the real word was... of course he did — were folded as though he had taken them off on purpose and laid them down.

But he hadn't.

He hadn't had the chance to do anything, least of all set his glasses up nice.

I went to pick them up but didn't because somebody must have done this, and the realization washed over me like a cold breeze. Ok, an animal could have come and licked the blood clean, got a little appetizer before its main course. That made sense. But no *animal could fold those arms – temples, shit – that way. Not a single one.*

I went back for the glasses alone, in the dark. Nobody knew I was coming because if they did, they would know I had a body in my trunk and maybe even how that body got there.

I was alone out there, and now it seemed darker than it was before, darker than when I let loose the shot that lit up the sky and blew up his head, darker than I've ever seen it before.

Was he still there... watching me?

Why did we always think it was a 'he', anyway? It could be a 'she' just as easily because there's some sick bitches out there too – just as sick as some of the dudes I know. It's ridiculous to just think men-

What the fuck? I hate when I got off on a tangent, thinking about something stupid instead of paying attention to the shit happening in front of me. Because somebody fucked

Karli ached. She flexed her fingers, stretching them, moving them out of the death grip they had been in as she squeezed the papers in her hands so tightly her fingertips turned white. The people around her seemed to have chosen their stories already, were starting to play with movement and work through the performances they were going to give center stage, yet she still sat flipping through the pages, looking for the one. She almost gave up and just picked one, wanted to so badly then because she wanted to have at least a few minutes to practice, but she couldn't do it. There was a story in there for her – she knew that as well as she knew her name. Karli also knew deep down that if she didn't find it, if she just went with something – anything – else, there would consequences.

Hypnopompia

The numbers spun – they spun! – right before my eyes and I know I'm groggy, I know I'm having trouble waking up this morning, but I know that's not right. When I woke and looked at my alarm clock, bastard that it is, beeping incessantly like a truck backing up, high-pitched and monotone at the same time... when I woke up and looked at the time, it was steady. 6:33 – I might have tried to ignore it for a few minutes and that's why it was 6:33 and not 6:30... sue me. It was overcast, but the sun was trying to peek through the blinds. I know that because I saw it. Everything was the way it usually was. Me not being able to haul my ass out of bed was normal too. Nothing to see here, folks, just your average Monday morning.

But I did get up. I didn't hit snooze this time. I trudged across the room like the walking dead, my eyes mere slits as I made my way to the bathroom, the commode, the sink, and then back into the bedroom. I sat down on the edge of the bed and put on the TV. A little news was what I needed, I thought, other voices in the room to coax me along. The distant thought I'd had last night about working out this morning was like a joke that some comedian had tried that fell flat. I had a moment to consider that I could dial my wake-up time back an hour if I was just going to let that fantasy go, felt the corners of my lips twitch in the beginnings of a smile at the thought before all was blank again. I fell asleep sitting up, remote in hand, and mouth wide open. I know that because I woke up that way too.

It couldn't have been long – couldn't have been. I would have fallen over or dropped the remote if it had been, right? Neither of those things had happened so I figured it had only been a few seconds, one of those moments where you doze off, are out of it so completely that you're disoriented when you wake up. I rolled onto my side, deciding to just give in, get another hour of sleep. I have a meeting in a few hours that I need to be sharp for and I was anything but that then. I laid down. Got into position to shut my eyes. That's when I saw it.

The guy on camera was talking about the weather – some

storm system coming from the north that will cool temperatures and make it feel like Christmas in July. His back was turned, so I couldn't see his face, but what I did see made me sit bolt upright. His suit jacket was slit up the back and so was his shirt. There was raw, pink flesh peeking out beneath all of it. I could see a huge blister between his shoulder blades.

The temperatures showed on the map. At first it was just local, but then the map expanded to the United States, and then to the world.

"It's 90 ºF in Calgary, but we're working on that. Parts of the US are hitting 175 ºF and temps in Nigeria topped 325 ºF last night. The Seine in Paris as well as the Canale Grande in Venice began to boil in the early morning hours. The Nile has boiled off completely, leaving lungfish and bolti to cook in the sun."

My mind couldn't process the words he was saying. I was distracted by the other data that was posted in the corners and running along the bottom of the screen:

Birds take flight in Florida only to burst into flames in the sky.

Woman fused to her car in Leeds.

Fissure opens in the ground to reveal lost ancient civilization beneath.

My mouth is open. I can hear myself panting.

The time on the screen, the one that I usually look at to confirm that I need to get up off my butt, get in the shower, and get going, was broken. The digital numbers were rolling, spinning, flying by. It was 6:45, then it was 7:22, then it was 3:14, then it was 5:58. It changed every second and it was driving me crazy. Every time I tried to look at it, pin it down, see it clearly, it was something different.

And the world boiled.

"Do you want to go back to sleep? It might be best to stay in bed, sleep it off and wake up dead."

Stuart knocking the chair over was so loud, it pulled Karli

out of the book, ripping her eyes from the words so force-fully that she wasn't sure she wasn't bleeding. She was irritated – beyond that… outright angry. She had finally found the story that spoke to her, the one that called to her from the pages. She wanted to keep reading, wanted to read to the end, felt like she had to or else… or else… she didn't know. Her fingers caressed the page she had been reading as her eyes searched the room for the cause of the noise, a veritable din seeming to rise from inside her as much as within the room.

Stuart was stumbling into the middle now, having righted himself after tripping over the desk chair combo that some school had donated to the cause. He had twisted his ankle in the fall, maybe even broken it, and it had blown up almost instantaneously, the swelling pushing straight the folds of his dingy sock, but he didn't seem to notice. He had announced his story title and then started acting it out right away, never waiting for the go ahead that Ms. Watson so loved to give, a practiced nod that was pretentions and demure at the same time. He barked the lines as if they had offended him and no one said a word.

The Conversation

"I don't want to go."

"What? Come on… you have to."

"Maybe I-"

"Maybe nothing. You already said you would – you can't just-"

"I said that years ago. I was a kid. He shouldn't have taken it so seriously. How could I say I would-"

"Wouldn't you?"

"Wouldn't I what?"

"Wouldn't you take it seriously? If you were getting everything you ever wanted, wouldn't you take it seriously?"

"How can he hold me to that, though? I was too young. It's-it's not..."

"Fair? Stop being ridiculous. There's no-"

"What are you talking about 'ridiculous'? How is it ridiculous? This is bullshit! I was too young to agree to something like that! No one in their right mind would hold me to-."

"- stupid."

"What? Why..."

"Are you kidding me right now?"

"I'm fucking serious. I'm not go-"

"And that's why I said you're stupid. He'll never go for it."

"Wha-"

"I mean, you know that, right? You can whine about how unfair it is and how you were too young, wah wah, but it's not gonna matter."

"You don't know-"

The girl with the oily hair and the dirty nose ring, the one Ms. Watson called Mara but whose name wasn't Mara at all, started shouting her story, her voice intermingling with Stuart's, not quite drowning his out, but matching it in volume and expression. And Stuart was doing what Ms. Watson told him too; he cried when his character cried. When he couldn't make real tears flow he made due, scratching at his eyes so that the blood would wet his cheeks just the same.

Stuart and Mara screamed their tales to each other from across the room, rupturing their vocal cords in grotesque harmony.

Penny candy loosely wrapped in dirty parchment paper. Lined up on a counter so caked with grime I could write my name in it. I did write my name in it after all, feeling like I had to, like it was the last thing I would ever do.

Stuckey wuz here.

I sighed as I looked at the parchment paper covering something that didn't look like candy at all. Too big. Too long. Too lumpy to be peanut brittle, like the man said it was. The man who was sweating and breathing heavy as he looked at me. The man whose fingers twitched as I watched. The day's special, he said, when I came into the store looking for some sunflower seeds. Try it, you'll like it. Something about the way he looked at me, about the way the door clicked when it closed, like it was locking me in, something about the haze in the dingy old everything store made me think I'd better try it if I knew what was good for me.

Penny candy loosely wrapped in dirty parchment paper. Waiting for me. Mine to eat. As much as I wanted. But I knew as my dry tongue tried to retreat down my throat, I would only be able to stomach one.

The floor was slick with things Karli didn't want to think about, couldn't let her mind linger on, not if she was going to get out of there alive. She could see the fluorescent light in the hallway flickering on and off, on and off, and she wished she was there under its artificial rays, skin turned sallow under the blue hue because if she was out there it would mean she had made it. It would mean she had escaped the orgy of death surrounding her and made it out, out of the room, out into the real world again where tentacles didn't caress the faces of the smitten and the ground didn't open up to swallow people whole. But Ms. Watson was between her and the door. And she had picked her story too.

7

SHE REMEMBERED everything about that day. The words, the gestures, the look in his eyes. None of the haze that covered old memories descended upon her, upon it. The day and everything that happened within it remained as clear to her as if she were living it that very moment.

"You can't show anybody the tape," she'd said when Riley walked into the living room holding the 8mm camcorder tape gingerly by its corners. He dangled it over her head where she sat on sofa, teasing her as she swiped at it. Her book fell off her lap and hit the floor, the thump sounding like a protest at the disruption. She had been reading the book they picked up at the used bookstore around the corner from their condo, the corner store that had just opened in the middle of their chic little created city in the burbs. He remembered that she had fallen in love with the book the moment she saw it, running her fingers along the cover as if it was some cherished family heirloom. She had opened it gingerly, turned the pages slowly, handling them only by the corners. It had gotten her a nod of appreciation from the owner who was running the checkout.

"You seem to know your way around old books," he had said, gesturing towards her with the practiced chin thrust of a Southern native.

"Not really," his wife had said honestly. He had never known her to own a book that she hadn't bought off the mass market paperback rack at the supermarket. "I just feel like I should be careful with this one. It seems… delicate."

"It might very well be," he mused, appraising the book from behind the counter as she held it out to him. "But I don't rightly know."

His wife had raised her eyebrows. It made him smile then as it did now.

"I got this from an estate sale," the kindly older gentleman continued, "I get a lot of my books that way."

"The person who owned it died?"

The man nodded. "And usually the family doesn't know what to do with all the junk that gets left behind. You'd be amazed how much we pack away over the years. So many books come from the recesses of someone's attic."

Riley had nodded along with them as he shopped, listening but not closely, enjoying the sound of the older man's voice more than he expected to.

"I buy them in bulk without ever looking at the titles. Truth be told, I enjoy the surprise when I go to unbox them and put them on my shelves."

The shopkeeper giggled.

His wife giggled.

He couldn't help but giggle too.

"You wanna give this one a whirl? It's beautiful, whatever it's about." The older man adjusted his glasses but saw no better for it. "*The Tales of Time*… catchy title, that one."

She had looked at the book in awe then—that's when he knew it was coming home with them.

"What's it about?" he asked, walking up behind his wife

and smiling at the shopkeeper. He had a few books of his own to buy and he laid them on the counter. Picking up the one on top, the shopkeeper mused, "Ah, one about Satchel Page... baseball fan, I assume?"

"That and history," he affirmed and kissed his wife on the cheek.

She was still holding the book when he asked again, "So, what's this one about?"

"I don't really know," she admitted, turning it over in her hands to find a back cover as empty as the front. "There's no information about what's inside anywhere."

"Maybe it *is* old. They didn't do summaries and such way back when," the shopkeeper supplied.

His wife thumbed the pages gently, looking for what, he wasn't sure. He started to ask her if there was something specific she was checking for when her voice filled his head. It was quick, fleeting, really, but he heard it. He toward her, a question on the tip of his tongue, when she spoke words that took shape in his own head as an echo,

"I saw him standing there
poise slightly mistook.
Stay away, my head tells me
but my heart beckons me look."

He felt the crease forming between his eyebrows, felt his lips purse as he formed the question, but he never gave it voice. Because it was gone... the words, the sense of déjà vu; it was completely gone. Riley tilted his head as he looked at his wife's unperturbed profile.

"How much do you want for it?"

The shopkeeper smiled, giving her a sum that he knew she would be happy with, and received the offered book to pack on top of the stack. She had smiled at him, then at the book now sheathed in the plastic bag, the unabashed excitement coloring her cheeks, making her look like a schoolgirl.

But she was no schoolgirl now.

Now she swatted above her head, grabbing at the video-tape he held just above her reach, like a hungry little bunny going after the perfect carrot. She raised herself from the sofa, once, twice, three times, trying to snatch the tape out of his hand. He loved the rise of her breasts against the cotton undershirt she donned on casual weekend mornings like that Saturday. They pressed against the shirt, her nipples hardening from the excitement of the game, the desire to win. They, unfettered by a bra, kissed when she dropped back onto the sofa, resting against her ribcage without argument. He dangled the tape again, a fourth time, longing to see the forbidden dance once more, but she didn't bite. Instead, she pouted playfully, her sensuality almost brimming over.

"Why can't I? We might be able to make money with this thing. Picture the ad: Hot, steamy amateurs play their naughty love games for all eyes to see. On sale at your nearest sleaze shop."

Melissa threw a pillow at Riley as he sat on the ottoman, hitting him on the side of his face. "You'd better not, if you know what's good for you," she said, turning her eyes back to the book waiting for her on the floor. Picking it up, she plucked an apple from the basket on the sofa table and settled back into her reading.

"I don't know, Mel. This might be a huge moneymaker for us. Can't you see the potential?" Riley asked slyly.

"Well, I don't know. I guess I'd have to see the tape first."

Riley made a spectacle of standing, bowing, and exiting the room, saying something like, 'Your wish is my command.' Melissa wondered why she couldn't remember exactly what he said. His exact words, that minor detail remained elusive to her, even though she had tried desperately to recall them over and over again. Their disappearance from her mind troubled her somehow, as if the answer to the question, the reason for the insanity that ensued a mere twenty-four hours after he spoke those words, was hidden within them. She became obsessed with them in the hours after his death, trying to conjure them up, to call them from the recesses of her mind. They held the secret, the knowledge. She became so sure of it that she could hardly think of anything else some days. Without those words, she felt the walls closing in around her, the air in the room thickening, constricting her throat, confining her. Without them, she felt the coldness of death on the back of her neck.

Melissa remembered, could visualize Riley bounding from the living room into the bedroom to retrieve the camcorder. He connected the cables easily, faster than she expected, so that the contents of the tape would appear on their television screen.

"I can't wait to see how this looks," he said, excitement seasoning his voice.

"You haven't even looked at it yet?" Melissa exclaimed as she rose to her knees on the plush sofa, her right hand wielding another pillow.

Riley covered his face with mocked terror as she threatened to throw the pillow, playfully imploring, "No, I haven't seen it yet, but I know it's awesome. I mean, you and me au naturel, our bodies entwined, in the throes of making love... It couldn't be anything but great. Now put the pillow down. You've got the arm of a major league baseball pitcher!"

...

Riley's laughter had been infectious.

Melissa let herself daydream, slipping into that formless bliss with the memory of it in her mind... a sound she hadn't heard in years... one she would never hear again. She came to wanting something. She went in search of it, knowing it was there, it hadn't left her, would never leave her. With a genuine pleasure that she hadn't felt since Riley, Melissa moved back to the sofa, treasure in hand. The same book she had been reading back then she had decided to start reading again that day, finding it in her closet waiting, just waiting for her to stumble upon it, to be enamored by it again.

The Tales of Time.

Melissa opened the book, savoring the smell of the old pages, warm and earthy. She felt the paper, like parchment, beneath her fingertips. She let it comfort her, reading the first page and losing herself within it.

$5.99

The movie went off and cycled back to the main screen, burning the stationary main page into the plasma TV more and more with every passing second. Carla had fallen asleep in front of the television again, as she had most nights since she got the DVD, unable to pull herself away from the screen to make it to bed. That really wasn't true though. She hadn't made it to bed because she didn't want to go to bed. She was right where she wanted to be.

Her sister thought she was crazy. Not literally, but she would have if she knew—if she believed. It wasn't like Carla hadn't tried to tell her, hadn't tried to share him with her... once... in the beginning. But Carla's sister didn't see it. He didn't speak to Tami the way he spoke to Carla. It was only right, really. He was Carla's, after all.

There wasn't anything special about the DVD, just a B-level movie with a cast that you think you might have seen before, but if so, you can't remember where. Carla got it out of one of those bins full of surplus movies discounted to $5.99.

But that wasn't all it was. Not to Carla.

The storyline was slow-paced and didn't really go anywhere, but Carla wasn't listening to the lines. The actors either never really "made it," were over-the-hill has-beens, or were newbies, but Carla recognized one of them. She should. She had seen him in her dreams for years.

Well, not him specifically, and not in the dreams like the ones you have when you're sleeping. But in her fantasies, in her daydreams, he was always there. He looked like a combination of her first love, a guy she knew from work, and the last guy she slept with. Such an odd mix, with unkempt hair, deep, penetrating eyes, the most sensuous lips. Carla could hardly tear her eyes away from the screen when he was in a scene and found herself reaching for the remote to fast-forward to his next one even if it meant she'd have no idea what was going on in the movie when she got there.

After her second time watching the movie all the way through he started talking to her.

At first it was just a look—he would look at the screen, seemingly at her, when he should have been looking at the actor opposite him. The first look was just a peek, just a glance; Carla almost didn't notice it at all. His second look was so much more meaningful. There was a playful twist to his lips that was endearing. His third look was downright obscene, the way he licked those luscious lips of his and lowered his eyelids. It gave Carla chills. The good kind.

Twenty minutes into the movie he spoke to her.

"Carla."

She felt as though she was waking from a dream when she heard her name. He was looking at her again, full on, shoulders squared to the screen—watching her. He was smiling just enough for her to see a hint of white from his teeth. She felt herself respond though she knew she shouldn't. He didn't have many lines in the movie; he was nothing more than a glorified extra, really, yet he had spoken her name as clearly as if he was sitting in the room whispering it in her ear. Carla spun her head around, looking in all corners of the room to be sure that he—that someone—wasn't there making fun of her, laughing at her expense. But she was alone.

With him.

She watched the movie three more times that day and more that weekend, blowing off shopping with her sister, a date with a guy she had been interested in for months, sleeping in her bed, and eating. With every viewing he said more to her, sometimes telling her how beautiful she was, pouting his lips as he spoke, letting her see all the curves and contortions they went through as they formed words, other times asking her to remove garments so he could see more. She felt silly and excited at the same time. It was weird, strange all of those things, but it was the best fantasy she'd ever had.

As Carla snored, catching her first reluctant winks in 30 hours, the screen flickered and blinked before finally catching again on the beginning of the movie. For a second, gone faster than Carla's eyes could have deciphered had she been awake, a roiling sea of red bubbled to the surface, washing Carla's face in blood as a tentacle reached out to stroke her cheek.

8

Upperville

UPPERVILLE. *The town where all the inhabitants are family. The town where nobody leaves because the world doesn't exist past the city limits. The town I'm from.*

Getting out was always a priority for me. The streams that border the town, the well that stood in our backyard, all smelled stagnant to me. Like rot. Like death. I didn't want to be consumed, to be sucked into the very ground like it was quicksand or the hungry mouth of a Venus Flytrap. I didn't want to live and die only knowing Upperville's monotony, with its white picket fences and its picturesque winding roads. "Upperville, the sleepy hollow less than an hour from the city," it had been called in some magazine years ago. To me it was more like "Upperville, town of the damned." So I left. I jumped on 66 and made for the city. Washington, DC.

I even wrote an article about it, one of my first features at the paper before I got moved up. "The Decline of Rural America," I called it, proudly typing Susan McCoy in the byline. I had to rewrite it so it didn't smack of Upperville bashing, not because I cared what the people back home thought—I didn't think they

71

would get the paper anyway, and if they did, they wouldn't read it —but because I wanted to make a good impression at my new job. When the paper came out there were grumblings, Mother said in her usual, I-just-happened-to-hear-it way. But there were always grumblings, at least, as far as I was concerned. People never seemed to like me or the things I did. Mother said it had more to do with her than it did with me, but she would never explain it. And she would never leave, no matter how much I begged. She said she was bound to the land just like my soul was bound to be free. I never listened when she started talking that way. Instead it strengthened my determination to get out. If that's what Upperville did to you, I didn't want any part of it. Sometimes Mother acted as kooky as the rest of them did. I wasn't going to let that happen to me.

I hate Upperville with a passion. Fucking Suckerville.

And now I'm going back.

Even my mother's death hadn't brought me back to that place. I had her body shipped to DC and forced anyone who wanted to pay their respects to leave their comfort zones and come to me. No one did. I found out later they held an informal service over my mother's body at the morgue. The coroner had lived in Upperville all his life, so even though it was against the rules, he lit a candle in front of mother's body on the slab along with the rest of them.

But now Bobby Zucker was dead. I had to go back.

The drive was over before I knew it. Memories of Bobby and me stealing kisses behind the school and copping feels in the cab of his father's pickup flooded my mind, wiping away the road and replacing it with his face. He was my first kiss, my first lover, my first love. I lived and breathed him until I left for college. He stayed behind to work at his father's hardware store. I begged him to come with me, to leave Upperville and start a life with me in the city. But he didn't. As the years passed and mother told me about Bobby's life —sending me the invitation Bobby gave her for his wedding to Mary Lou Kramer, (a cowgirl if there ever was one), giving me baby pictures when his children were born—I couldn't believe I had been so wrong about him. He wasn't the person I thought he was, wasn't the free spirit who thought for himself and did what he wanted to do in life. He was just like the rest of them in Upperville: a drone.

But I never forgot about him.

Even with all the dating I did, all the near misses, I never forgot about Bobby. I always wondered what it would have been like had he left Upperville and come with me. He might have been a lawyer, like he wanted to be. He might have had a successful practice in Northwest, DC, might have been a real player. We might have been happy.

But now he's dead.

Carlene, my mother's best friend and the only other person in Upperville who knew how to reach me, said that he fell from a ladder and hit his head. She said he never regained consciousness, using a sympathetic tone that made it seem like that was for the best. But it wasn't. The Bobby I knew would have wanted to wake up and say goodbye to his family and friends, would have wanted one last moment to see the sun from his window. But I kept that to myself. There was no sense in upsetting Carlene's 'Uppervillian' logic, her untested, all-knowing sensibility.

Damn him for making me come back.

Damn him for not coming with me.

The main road—aptly named Main Street—looked the same as it had when I took it out of town twenty-one years ago. Same old stores, looking the worse for wear in the diminishing light, the same old church at the end of the badly pocked street. People went about their normal routine as I drove by, talking with each other in the entrance to the post office while scratching at their oversized, dirty overalls and plaid shirts, tipping their hat to the old woman who strolled past. Doing nothing. I've seen it all before. It hurt to think that Bobby had become one of them.

The funeral home was off a side street with even more cars lined up than on Main. People had come to pay their respects.

Bobby must have been well-liked, and why wouldn't he be? He was one of the most handsome kids in school, one of the most grounded people I had ever met. I bet he was a magnet, someone who the cowpokes wanted to be around. It made them feel better about themselves. And now that beacon was gone.

That's what he was, wasn't he? A beacon that had called me back to a place I swore I'd never step foot in again.

With a deep breath, I walked into the funeral home. It was suitably muted, as were most places like that—no sense in turning up the lights so you can see the death mask in plain view.

I didn't recognize Carlene when she approached me. "Susan? Is that you? My God, you look so different!" she cackled louder than she should have in a funeral home.

"Carlene. It's great to see you!" I lied. I didn't care if I ever saw her again. Bobby was the only person I cared about in that godforsaken town. And now he was gone.

Two other people milled behind her, openly listening to our exchange. "Well, you remember Karen Whitetower and Vern Glover, don't you?"

I nodded my greeting, desperately wanting to get away from them.

"I bet you're anxious to see Bobby, then," she said, her face twisting in a sly smile. "I know how close you two were."

Something about her troubled me.

"He's right in there," she said, turning my shoulders and nudging me toward the room where Bobby's body lay. "Go on," she urged, flashing her too-sweet smile.

The whole drive there all I wanted to do was see him, see that Bobby was dead with my own eyes, but now that I was there, in the place where he was laid out, I was afraid. Seeing him would mean that it was really over. Everything we had ever shared was done, gone, finished. Even when he got married, I thought there might be a little something left, something we might grab onto later in life.

But now that he was dead, there would be no chance of that. I was terrified.

"Go on, Susan," Carlene said, her voice more urgent this time. "Go in and see Bobby."

I started walking before I allowed my thoughts to register. Carlene's behavior, her expressions, everything about her bothered me. Why did she care if I went in to see Bobby? Why did it have to be so rushed? I brushed the concern away, chalking it up to my nervousness. I was, after all, at my first love's funeral. Maybe I was a little sensitive.

I heard the whispering among the people who ringed the corridor—

"That's Lizzie's girl, isn't it?"

"She ain't been back here for twenty years!"

"Not even for her mother's funeral."

I turned to see who made that comment, but no one met me eye to eye. Funeral? I had mother's funeral in DC. If they were talking about their cultish sendoff in the morgue, fine. But they said funeral. Had they held a service that I missed? Anger welled within me, swirling inside my stomach. How dare they not let me know about something like that? I'll have to ask Carlene about that before I leave, I thought as I turned their whispers around in my head. I approached Bobby's casket at a snail's pace.

It was open, with a yellowish light shining on the place where Bobby's head should have rested. But there he wasn't there. I didn't see the what I expected to see, Bobby with his eyes closed and the lids pulled a little too tightly over the eyes to look natural, Bobby with makeup dusting his temples to cover the greenish gray tint his flesh had taken in death, Bobby whose glued lips looked nothing like the soft ones I had kissed so long ago. I picked up my pace, ignoring the voice in my mind that insisted that Bob's body laid lower than usual, that his wife must have sprung for the deluxe model casket, high walls, plush satin and all.

No casket is that deep, a stronger, more resilient version of my own voice admonished.

He wasn't there.

The casket was empty, its silk bedding untouched. As I turned to ask the nearest Upperville moron what was going on, I caught sight of a stocky man, about six feet tall with dusty brown hair and twinkling brown eyes. Bobby. He was older, but I'd know his face anywhere.

"Bobby, what—?" I started to ask him. His smile spread into a wild grin as I shrank against the casket. I never saw who hit me in the back of the head, never even felt the blow. The blood running down my neck felt warm, calming as I rested my head on the pillow and looked at Bobby. I didn't feel them hoist my legs over the side of the casket, didn't hear them laugh and jeer, condemning me for leaving as I bled out. Only the touch of Bobby's lips on mine registered. When he parted my lips and put his tongue in my mouth I closed my eyes like I did when we were kids.

MORBID… that's what it was. Not to mention creepy and coincidental as hell. Casey didn't like that the story she had just read kinda sorta mirrored her life right now. But that's what she got for picking up a book that someone left behind and sticking her nose into it, right? It's just that the book was so interesting—so vintage looking—that she was drawn to it. The colors, maroon and gold, antique brushed or something. The feel of the cover was cool too—soft and velvety like the inside of those boxes that held chips and dice for a home poker set. Weird that she would compare it to that but there it was, her days of playing dealer at the kitchen table in her mother's house had been good for something after all. But it was exactly right, no matter how obscure of a reference it might be. That's how the cover felt under her hands. She couldn't stop herself from rubbing it one way and then the next just to feel the microfibers shift. Her boyfriend used to call her a hipster because of shit like that. Maybe he was right.

But he wasn't calling her shit anymore, was he? He wasn't calling anyone anything, and never would. He was dead. That's why she was sitting on that godforsaken bus heading into the hills of West Virginia. She was going back home to say goodbye to her first love, the first in a long string of assholes.

He had kicked off early, the bastard. He was supposed to wait for her to come back and make it right.

Casey wouldn't have even known he was dead if it wasn't for her cousin texting her on the sly. Nobody wanted her back in town; nobody wanted her near Len, even as he lay dead at Johnson's Funeral Home. She had taken off without saying goodbye and most people thought that was fine enough. Casey and her city ways had never been understood out there in the one stoplight town she was from. Her moving on was expected, and it was fine and dandy to them. She told them she wouldn't claim that po-dunk shithole when she made it big, and they nodded approval. The way things were going for her, no one would have to worry about that anyway.

She had moved on, sure, had her share of guys to pass the time. But Len was the one, and she knew it. Her cousin knew it. Len's bitch of a wife knew it, too. As soon as she could get her shit together, as soon as she could call herself fit to help raise Len's two little girls, she was going to go back and take what was hers. But the cancer got there before she was ready. And now none of that mattered anymore.

Casey fondled the book on the bus as she rode into town; she handled it as she watched the ceremony from the doorway of the little church, away from the eyes of people who would spit on her as easily as look at her. She kept it in her hand, rubbing at the velvet hard enough to wear it smooth as she looked over at the mound of dirt waiting to be pushed in the hole as soon as the stragglers left the graveside. His mother was still there, his sister too. And that bitch of a wife who would forever and always be able to call Len hers.

Ten.

Twenty.

Thirty minutes passed while she waited for everyone to clear out. She only wanted a minute with Len, just one last minute to tell him she was sorry she left him behind.

She opened the book in her hands, the only thing that had grounded her since she started on her journey back to Hell. And she read.

Cemetery Road

I've never been afraid of the dark, but I'm damned scared now. Donnie said the trees looked like legs in the dark, and he was right. My flashlight ain't helpin' things either, just makes 'em look like they're moving.

I don't know why I'm here but I am.

I know'd better than to come up here, but I dint use the sense God gave me. They was just talking so much shit about how I wasn't gonna do it and how I was a chicken shit, that I just had to. So I'm here, and I wish I wasn't.

I drove up to the corner, like they said to, and parked the car. They said they'd be watching to see if I would do it, so I followed every instruction. I dint want them to say I cheated. And I damned sure don't want to do it again. I started walking up the road and zipped up my jacket. It was cold as hell outside, no kind of weather to go playing around in a cemetery, but then again, when was? My footsteps sounded loud as I walked up the deserted road, not a car to be seen. I started to count the crunching of the rocks—made the time go by quicker. By the time I got to 150, I had made it up the hill and could see the headstones shining off my flashlight. The white ones seemed to glow.

Houses lined the street, every one of them with dark windows. Who the hell would want to live across the street from a cemetery anyway? Even if it doesn't spook you, it ain't nothing to look at. The only people ever outside are crying.

Six, maybe seven houses stood there and nobody in any of 'em. For some reason that don't set right with me.

I looked at the tombstones, trying to decide if I was going in or not. My granddaddy's stone was on the edge of the street, damned near paved over when they put up the new road back in '84. It leaned to the side, sunken in the ground, chunks taken out of it from the wind and rain. Just beat up. That's what's gonna happen to me, I thought as I stared at it sticking out of the ground like a broken tooth. Something about that made me want to run.

I looked back at the houses with their black eyes staring at me. I couldn't tell which one I felt safer having my back to. The cold made me decide quick.

I looked back to the cemetery and saw the same tombstones, the same trees, and decided to go in. Ain't no difference in a cemetery in the day or at night. Dead people there all the time, and they can't bother nobody. And anyway, Donnie and the guys're watchin'.

The first step inside was hard, but they got easier after that. I walked past granddaddy's grave and on down the Barlow line, ending up by my cousin who just got put in the ground a couple months back. I snickered at his grave and thought for a second about leaving that $5.00 I owed him on the grass, but nah. Why waste good money on someone who can't use it anymore? Poor sucker.

This shit is easy, once you get the balls to do it. I walked around like I owned the place. Thought about what it might cost to buy a place like this. Make money off putting people in the ground? You could stack three or four coffins on top of each other and charge for a single plot! Do that over so many acres, and you got a goldmine. Might need to look into it tomorrow when I get up.

I figured that was enough after I got to Sandy Laurelton's grave. Old biddy died back in 1837 at the age of, what was it, 96? I think that's what the cross said, but it was pretty splintered, so I could be wrong. Either way, old is old. I gave the back of Sandy's cross a slap like she'd probably never had on her ass when she was alive and started back the way I came, happy this shit is over. I dare them to talk shit about me now.

When I saw them coming I couldn't help but call out. And why did it matter anyway? Dead people don't care how loud you are.

"Hey Donnie!" I yelled, steam filling up the air like a white cloud. "I did it, dude! Smacked this little bitch on the ass, too."

I thought Donnie would get a kick out of that. Hell, he's the one who likes to fuck 'em when they're damned near dead anyway. But he dint say anything. Well fuck him then, the jealous little bitch. I probably stayed in longer than him, and he was pissed. So who's the chicken shit now?

I stopped walking and let them get closer, the cloud in front of my face going in and out as I caught my breath. They dint have a cloud in front of theirs.

9

"IT's like it's the 60s or something, me asking for a house call," Justina said to the empty room as she rubbed the sides of her arms, but she couldn't think of anything else to do. Her son hadn't been eating- he hadn't been bathing… he had barely come out of his room in three days. He had been relieving himself where he sat for the last day, only moving enough to switch out sheets of paper after the yelling stopped. Once he'd spent himself, shouting about the candy that was waiting for him at the corner store, the candy he'd read about over the old lady's shoulder, he'd fallen silent, offering no explanation to his mother; just letting the words sit in the air between them, fat and pungent.

He was freewriting again, like he had when he was young and none of the words made sense. They didn't make much more sense now, not all of them. There was a poem about a woman looking for a black dress to bury her daughter in and an apparition visiting a young woman on the cusp on marriage. She couldn't figure out where it was all coming from: neither Justina or her son had ever written poetry before or even read it except in school, and even though that doesn't mean much of anything, all that eloquence surprised her. Her son wasn't that kind of guy, at least she hadn't thought so until she read his words. While it was nice to think he had been sitting on a talent like that all this time, doing something more than just playing videogames all day, the words didn't feel right. They didn't feel like they were his. Justina didn't know what that could mean.

And the way he looked while he was doing it... it had made her retreat from the room more than once. He was staring at something off to the right, his eyes upturned to see something in the corner, something invisible to her but that held his attention even when she called his name. His jaw was slack, and his breathing was slow and deep. She'd held her own breath once to listen for his, his chest rising and falling so infrequently that she became worried.

And then there was the mumbling.

As unintelligible as it was, more sounds than words, it was spooky to her, scary in a way that she couldn't define. Justina told the doctor about it when they spoke, deciding to call after the stench had made its way out of his room and into the hallway. He was too big to move—he had reached his full height long ago and towered over her, not to mention outweighing her by 80 pounds. He was a man now, and she feared that he would be mortified if he snapped out of his fugue to find his mother wiping his behind.

By the time the doctor got there three new sheets of paper had been filled, writings about an old woman who fell down the stairs and broke her neck; a man who stepped into oncoming traffic and had gone through the windshield of a car; a dog that ran circles on his person's grave. There were poems about people in the woods, lost loves in the distance, straddling the line between life and death. The words were all over the page, up one side and down another, front and back, spiraling in the corners to break out into pieces and fray at the ends. Red, red letters on death and dying and loss and darkness written in blood. There were letters left for her, penned in what spilled with a sloppy hand, and she couldn't bear to read them herself or even lay eyes on them. She screamed as the doctor read the first out loud, unaware of the inscription, the dedication, her son's final request ignored. The doctor read the words like he didn't understand them, not separately, nor in combination.

Peering into the darkness
I have a sense of one
with me
searching also
for themselves
but finding me.

And Justina screamed and screamed because the words made no sense, no sense at all, and they made complete sense and she was sorry, so very sorry that her happy boy would never be like before again... that he would never be.

10

"WHERE ARE you heading off to looking like you just stepped out of *GQ*?" Charlene said. She always had a nice word for the boys, flirting with them even though she was pushing 70. Because 70 isn't dead... only dead is dead and she would look and flirt and pinch and get a taste if someone would let her until she *was* dead. Once you got there, there was no going back. She planned to enter the gates of Heaven with no regrets.

"More like *Popular Mechanics*, if you ask me," Walter said, coming into the office from the loud bus garage, scratching the dandruff off his balding head. He appraised the younger man for a moment and then, finding a legitimate spot on his face— a little grease from the garage that had worked its way into the skin beneath his eye, and taken residence there—he took joy in saying, "You—you might want to get that before you go out, lover boy."

Charlene and Walter laughed when he ran to the mirror and wiped frantically at his face. "You got a date or something?" Charlene asked as her laughter waned and she moved to refill her coffee cup. It would be her fourth of the day, and her shift hadn't even really gotten started good.

"Meetin' her parents today," he said, still checking himself over in the mirror.

"Well, don't forget this," Charlene said, her tone leaning toward fond. She held out the book he had put in his box, giving it over reluctantly. It felt good in her hand. The cover was velvety soft and the pages, they smelled good...old in a smart kid of way, not a dirty one. Even though she wasn't much for reading, she wanted to open the book and see what was inside. Were the words written in that old English script they used to use way back when? Were some of the letters embossed in gold?

He took the book and tucked it under his arm possessively.

"Where'd you get that, anyway?"

"My bus," he replied, hoping he didn't have to say much more. Keeping stuff they found on the bus wasn't frowned upon if you did it after a few days—as long as you gave the person who left it behind time to pick it up from the lost and found. But he saw the book after his morning route and snatched it up right away. It was the perfect thing to give her mother; he knew that right on the spot. It looked formal, proper. She would think he was smart. Maybe she wouldn't give him such a hard time about driving a bus. It was just a temporary thing, anyway...

Walter was about to say something stupid—something that would take the wind right out of his sails. Charlene knew that like she knew her own name. Guys like Walter, the ones who gave up on love and life and anything outside of the four walls they worked and lived in always tried to clip the wings of the ones who didn't.

She cut him off before he could say anything at all, talking too loud and not caring one whit about it, "I think she'll like it. It's fancy. Got a real nice feel to it."

"Yeah," the younger man said, hoping she could see the thanks in his eyes.

Charlene looked at him for a minute longer before shooing him out. "Don't want to be late to meet the Mama. Go on, get out of here. We'll see you in the mornin'!"

He left, and Charlene smiled at the door after he was gone. Walter laughed and shook his head as he left the office for somewhere back in the recesses of the garage.

When he got in his car he froze. He was nervous. As much as he wanted to tell himself that meeting her mother wasn't a big deal, he knew it was. He didn't know if he wanted to meet her—didn't know if he wanted to put himself through it all. She would ask where he was from, would ask what college he went to, would ask what he wanted to do with the rest of his life. He didn't have answers to any of those questions—at least not answers that he thought she would be satisfied with. *Where are you from?* Bumfuck, USA. *Did you go to college?* Yeah, I started up at the community college but just stopped going. *What do you want to do with the rest of your life?* Not drive a bus, I'll tell you that much, but apart from that, not sure. Bullshit, all of it—truthful, but worthless... except maybe that last answer. He didn't have a clue what he wanted to do today, let alone tomorrow. He knew that was true—did his girlfriend know that too?

He really didn't want to go.

He sighed and thumbed open the book, chuckling to himself about who he was and where his life was headed. Of course the mom would hate him. He was too cheap to even buy the woman a gift, had to steal one off the seat of his bus. Because that's what it was, right... stealing? Someone might come back for it—someone had obviously left it there, and whoever it was had taken care of it. It was obviously old, maybe even some kind of antique or something, yet the binding wasn't broken; the cover wasn't scuffed. He thought fleetingly of selling it—it could be worth a lot of money. But no. Someone riding the bus—especially his route today... the one that went to the sticks—wouldn't be carrying a book that was worth a lot of money. Someone owning a book like that was likely riding in a Rolls Royce and getting carted around by a driver wearing those fancy black gloves.

The book was worthless... just like him.

"Let's see what kind of impression we can make together," he said aloud to the book within the confines of his empty car. He went to close the book but caught sight of a story called "Family Dinner." He could almost hear his name being called from the yellowed pages.

Family Dinner

"You gotta be kidding me," Nick said as he turned onto the dark road... a road that looked just like the last one, and the one before. He had been driving for an hour into the deep woods and across state lines for a girl he had just met. Come to dinner, she had whispered in his ear the week before. Meet my family.

Already?

They had only been out on a few dates, had only spent maybe 7 hours together, but who's counting? She talked about cavern hunting (who can resist stalactites and stalagmites?) and great skiing when he got there, but that wasn't the reason he said yes. It was her. She wore such a sweet smile when she asked him to come, looked so perfect in her tight jeans and loose sweater. She felt so warm when he hugged her close and felt her form underneath all that knit, so he said sure. It didn't matter that her family dinner was the same day that he was celebrating a win with his buddies, sending him in the other direction from her folks' house and adding 45 minutes to an already long drive.

Amy.

All that mattered was the smile she would greet him with when she opened the door and the warm hug that waited for him.

Assuming he could ever get there.

The drive from Fairfax was the easy part. He knew his old stomping grounds well enough to make it most of the way out of Northern Virginia and over to Warrenton, where the city lights were a distant memory, but that was as far as he could go without help. It didn't help that there was no Interstate to get onto. The closest one would have put him a half hour out of his way, so he braved the side streets and back roads, relying on his GPS and, after a while, instinct. GPS, God love it. Such a great tool when it works. But like that early-adopt model he won at a casino in the late 90s, the one that had to be suction cupped to his windshield and that sent him into the Baltimore harbor every time he made a turn off Pratt St., the route his phone gave him was no use. It kept rerouting as if the mountains surrounding the sleepy hamlet grew up overnight, making a once usable road impassible. Nick had gotten so sick of hearing that unaccented, mild-mannered female voice telling him to make a U-turn, that he closed the app.

White's Taxidermy on his left. Margie's Good Eats on the right. Coincidence?

Nick would have laughed at his joke if he hadn't already told it before. He was sure he passed a similar combination a few towns back. Taxidermist Tull and Jake's Steak. Forever Pets Taxidermy and The Rib Shack. It was funny the first time, but not anymore.

Nick pulled into a gas station. He was happy to find one of those big chain stations like the ones he was used to at home. The drive itself was starting to look like one of those low-budget horror movies. He didn't need to add a broken down, one-pump station with the stereotypically grimy gas jockey to the mix. He and three other people filed into the brightly lit convenience store at the station. He listened as the person in front of him asked for directions to the ski lodge near where Amy's family lived—the same one that had a hot chocolate with his name on it waiting by a warm fire. The route sounded like the one he had just come off, long and twisty and dark. When it was his turn, Nick told the attendant— young and clean, thank you very much—that he was looking for directions to the same place.

"But where's the highway?" Nick asked after being given the same directions the woman before him got. "There's gotta be something that cuts through these mountains instead of sticking to the back roads." He picked up a candy bar and laid it on the counter. "I feel like I've been driving around forever."

The young man nodded imperceptibly, his eye twitching under the patch of oily hair visible beneath the rim of his red service cap. "I wish, but there's nothing like that," he said a little too eagerly. "This is the best way to get out to the ski lodge, especially since it's almost dark."

Nick smiled at him incredulously. That's why he wanted the highway! The afternoon light was fading fast, and he did not relish the idea of driving around the woods on winding roads in the dark. He did not want hitting a deer to be in his future.

"There's gotta be something. I mean, there's no way trucks take these narrow streets to deliver to you. What do they use?"

The attendant rang up his candy bar without looking at him.

Nick tried again. "I saw lights, but I couldn't get to them."

Giving Nick his change, the attendant said, "I don't know. But the directions I gave you will get you to the ski lodge in about 2 hours."

The attendant held out his bag with hands that looked like they could be shaking. Just a little, but it was there. Nick shook his head, thanked him, and got back in the car. Two hours? He'd been driving for an hour already, and the GPS said it was just about 2 hours away from where he started. Could he really be that far off course?

Nick looked in the direction that the attendant told him to go. Two of the three cars that came in with him headed that way. The other car, a guy in a button-down shirt open at the neck and dress slacks driving a non-descript black sedan that screamed company car, went the other way. Nick climbed into his own car and turned it on fast. He could feel the attendant's eyes on him, beseeching him to go the way he had been told, but Nick ignored the sensation as it crept up his back to caress his neck. He followed the company car even as the gas station attendant screamed, "No!"

Leafless trees.

Asphalt.

Dead grass.

Repeat.

There was nothing. Not even a boarded-up house to break up the monotony. Nothing at all. Nick had caught up with the other rebel and was right behind him. The man had even made a saluting gesture to him in his rearview mirror – just two compadres bucking the system. It was getting late. At 4:30, it was almost completely dark. There were no streetlights on the country road, but Nick could see some off in distance. The road traversed a lazy hill. If he could just get down to those lights, Nick was sure he'd find a way to cut through the spiderweb of back roads and take him where he needed to be. Amy's family lived in a college town—there were bound to be major routes leading to it. He just needed to find one.

Oh crap, Amy!

She had to be worried. Nick picked up his phone and noticed she had called twice already. When? He had the phone with him when he was in the gas station, and it had been sitting in the cupholder the whole time he was driving. It never rang.

"Technology," Nick said out loud, "Gotta love it."

Nick dialed Amy's number and heard nothing. No ringing, no beeping, no 'all circuits are busy' message—nothing.

He looked at his phone, taking his eyes away from the road for a second to see if he had missed a number somehow. He had just added her number to his favorites list, but now he wondered if he had put the number in wrong. Nick didn't see the front end of the company car disappear like it got sucked through an invisible *portal. The man threw the car in reverse and it lurched backwards. The doors seemed to stretch, pulling away from the side panels as if running from a magnet. The metal pulled like saltwater taffy, stretching in long lines of silver and black. The back tires spun against the asphalt, digging for purchase but finding none.*

Nick didn't hear the tires screeching on the road, nor the muted screams left behind like an echo as the man travelled through the barrier. He didn't notice the country road rippling as it engulfed the non-descript sedan, the facade rising and falling like paper in the wind to reveal a glimpse of a black core that seemed to pulse with life. He never saw how flat the landscape was, how it mirrored itself every few yards, like cheap floor tiles keeping pattern. Instead, he heard the unaccented, mild-mannered female voice of his GPS telling him to turn around to start route guidance, only this time she was screaming.

11

THE MOVIE WAS GOOD.

It had been a long time since she'd gone to a drive-in theater, and she was loving every minute of it. She only wished they still had the tinny speakers they could put on the windows, all the cars connected by a webwork of thick cords attached to sound pillars mounted throughout the lot the way they did back in the day instead of the audio shooting through the car speakers. She remembered those days, when she and her mom would check to see what movie was playing—and by check she meant leaning their heads over to look at the screen that stood tall opposite the supermarket to see what was on. If they liked what they saw, they would drive over and buy tickets, park their station wagon in one of the spots, and share the pint of ice cream that was in one of the grocery bags. If they had seen that particular movie before but really liked a few scenes, well, they weren't beyond pulling up to the fence and watching the screen sans speakers... and sans tickets.

So what, she was retro, old school? There was something

to be said for the simplicity of the world before technology ruled.

The scene onscreen was epic. There was a fire, one that the characters had somehow missed before it was raging, the smell of smoke, let alone the heat, not registering until it was too late. Kelsey stared at John with such sweet understanding that he wanted to look away. But he couldn't do it, not when he knew he was looking into her eyes for the last time.

She felt like she was part of the scene, on set, listening in: right there.

When he saw her last she was reading a book, a story about a zombie apocalypse or something—that much he had picked up from looking over her shoulder. They were closing in, people in the house were already dead, and the one guy left was running around, thinking about what he should take from the home he knew he would never return to. It was good, this story by some anonymous author, and John wanted to finish it, felt compelled to do so, to rush past where Kelsey was in the story and speed-read the remaining pages, but then his phone rang with his sister on the other end sounding frantic. John removed himself from the room where Kelsey remained with the book to find out what new hell his sister was embroiled in, vowing to come back to the story as soon as they were done talking. Because zombies were at the window and John had to find out if the kindly doctor would make it out alive. But when he got back, the room was fast on its way to being engulfed in flames.

"You wouldn't let go of the book," John said through the tinny speakers. "I—I couldn't pry it out of your hands."

His voice was filled with desperation because Kelsey's sundress had succumbed to the flames right away, leaving her skin bare and vulnerable. The yellow flames licked around her arms, seeming to cut through her, teasing as they devoured. Kelsey still held the book in her hand, clasping it to her chest even as the flames reached toward it… much like she was holding the old, dusty book she found under the seat of the car when she bought it at auction the day before. She had meant to throw it away—it smelled of something she couldn't place but that unsettled her nonetheless—but it was still there, had been lying on the passenger seat where she had left it. The only reason she was holding it now was because her boyfriend was sitting there watching the movie… more like sleeping there during the movie. The book had sat between them when he got in the car during the ride to the drive-in, but when he fell asleep and the movie started getting good, she reached for it where it sat perched on her gear shift.

She didn't think about it, not when Kelsey's infatuation with her own book bloomed in the movie; not when it controlled every aspect of her existence… not even when the flames licked at it but it wouldn't catch.

People onscreen were running and she could detect movement in her peripheral own vision.

Directions were being bellowed, seeming to surround the car, coming from inside and outside of it, impossibly amplified.

There was so much noise. The sound director must have gone all out on the mix because she could hear crackles, hissing, popping, sizzling. Combine that with the yelling and screaming, the crying and sobbing, the muted beating that sounded like water hitting glass, intermittent thumps that seemed to come from another world, and you had an idea of what she was hearing. Stellar work, this. She tried to remember the name of the movie and found that she could not. She couldn't remember what town she was in or whether or not she'd bought popcorn when she got there.

She had to pee, so she did.

On screen, Kelsey's lips were turning a painful red.

"The book said you would do this," Kelsey said, her voice on its way to a ruin John hoped he didn't have to hear. "Either that or—" Flames danced along her shoulders and reached toward her hair.

"Or I would."

Kelsey faltered, failing. Dying.

Her boyfriend woke up to the heat of fire burning his lungs. He found himself locked in the car with his girlfriend who was just staring at the movie screen like she didn't smell the smoke threatening to force them into unconsciousness, like she didn't know there was a raging fire in the backseat.

The heat was starting to irritate the skin on the back of his neck.

"Hey! Honey, what the fuck?" he yelled as he slammed himself against the door. "Unlock the door—we need to get out of here."

The flames blazed unexpectedly fast. He beat his fists, his elbows, his hands against the glass, but it wouldn't shatter.

"I finished it, honey," she started, her voice nothing more than an afterthought now that the flames had leapt into her hair, "I finished the story, and it was everything I could ever hope for."

He screamed, wailed, really, as he saw her go up in flames, eyes open, staring at the movie screen while speaking to him in a monotone voice he had never heard her use before, all the while clutching the book in her hands. He hadn't seen her toss a match into the jumble of clothes and bags and junk strewn on the backseat—things she had purchased from a day of shopping in her new-to-her car. He wasn't awake when the flames grew behind them as she watched the screen, burning the image of the movie into her head as she mirrored the character's fate. All he knew was that somewhere along the line the screw that he always thought had been loose in her fell out, and he missed it, missed all the signs—might have ignored them so he could keep enjoying her for a little while longer. And now... well, now his time had run out.

On screen, John hesitated—his body telling him to run, to get blankets and beat the flames away, but his mind forcing him to stay. He knew she was gone. It was his duty to stand with her and watch until the very end.

"Kiss me," Kelsey croaked and reached for her boyfriend on the screen. Inside the car, she reached for her boyfriend too, saying the same words Kelsey had in the movie. And she was beautiful. The way the flames haloed her head, the way the orange made her face look like it was glowing... only she wasn't glowing, she was burning, and he could smell her, and she was reaching for him, and how was that possible... how was it possible that she hadn't passed out yet? How the fuck was it possible that she was awake through all of this?

She always had the nicest lips, he thought. That was the first thing he noticed and would be the last thing he would ever think about once she had her way with him. He was thinking that when she picked him up to go to the movies. She had been reading the last few sentences of a story in the very book she clutched in her death grip—the book that didn't seem to be burning even though it was embroiled in flames.

"... wanting closure; wanting release," she had read out loud. "The orange glow, tinged with the faintest lick of blue, she knew, would give her peace."

The way her mouth formed the words, stretching, pulling, pouting—it drove him mad. That's why he could never look at her when she spoke, could never stop himself from pressing his own mouth to hers, capturing her lips in a worshipping kiss. But right then, as her lips were curling over the words she spoke, caressing them, savoring them as if a last meal, the flames licked into her mouth to dance with her tongue.

John was hypnotized by the scene—the flames, the smell of burning flesh in the air, all of it like the sway of a boat on the open sea. It was intoxicating the way Kelsey's visage seemed to undulate in front of him, to waver like the air over asphalt in the summer heat. He stood watching as Kelsey's arm rose to touch his face.

She was engulfed in flames—pretty much the whole car was—but she was smiling at him. Not smiling, no, not really, he noticed as he leaned closer, abandoning the idea of escape in lieu of moving toward her. She was smirking, one corner of her mouth pulling up knowingly as she stared at him… beckoned him. That one side of her face had burned away, the sinews and muscles drawing up to reveal the bone beneath, escaped him. He was too busy looking at the side of her mouth that had remained untouched, those lips he so loved to kiss, to nip, to suck… he was too busy remembering how those lips felt on his skin to notice that she was dying in front of him. Dying and reaching out to him. She closed the distance between her flaming self and his sweat-soaked shirt in a second.

He recoiled just a little too late.

Her burning hand touched her boyfriend's chest as Kelsey's touched John's face, leaving a flame that would devour his cheek. She was distantly aware that her mind had been taken over by something—some evil being that wanted this, that craved the destruction. She could smell her own flesh burning and knew she should have lost consciousness by now, but still she was awake, even as her boyfriend screamed and writhed. She willed it to happen; tried to exert power over herself just one more time and force her eyes closed. But she couldn't. The thing inside her—the thing that had forced her to read the book, to hold onto it for dear life as the flames enveloped her, the car, the wire connecting the tinny speaker to the sound post between the quad of spaces she was slotted in, the same one that short circuited from the heat and sent sparks into the now empty cars that shared it— was too strong. The thing… it always got what it wanted, and right now it wanted her to take her boyfriend with her, to kill him just like Kelsey killed John in the movie that would be the last thing she would ever see.

She ran her hand around to the back of her boyfriend's head and pulled him toward her as his shrieks and sighs died down and he succumbed. She latched on to him, needing to feel him close as she waited to die as well. Her voice, nothing more than a painful whisper now, broke free as she embraced him with one arm, still refusing to let go of the book, but she doubted he heard her. He was burning in earnest now, the fire having spread from his shorts to his shirt to his hair with immeasurable speed.

"I love you, baby," she said again, at last slumping against the seat as the fire ravaged her throat, burst her eyeballs, and stilled her tongue.

12

Sunday Morning

HE STOOD ON THE STEPS, listening to the choir lift their voices, a last-minute practice before the morning's service. He wished he could plug his ears, blot out the sound with his screams, something. He didn't want to hear them thanking God for their lot in life, for the streets that stank like piss and vomit, for the bread and milk the government let them have for free. He didn't want to open those heavy doors and feel the oppressive heat greet him. It was cooler outside. He didn't want to smell the foyer, its odd mixture of incense, sweat, and sulfur ever present. He couldn't bring himself to bow his head in supplication again. He didn't feel anything when he did anyway—just the hot, sticky sweat that coated his neck cooling in the air that had been whipped up by the dirty fan propped in the window.

But he had to.

Just as sure as he knew his own name, he knew he had to enter that place, hear those sounds, and smell those smells again. The thick, glossy tenement paint that caked the walls had his name etched in it. The hymns that the choir wailed incessantly spoke to him this time... every time. At least that's what it felt like. He was afraid of what would happen if he didn't respond to their deafening call.

He opened the doors to the church—big hulking things made of dark wood with antique gold trim—and slipped inside. He didn't want to make a sound, didn't want to draw attention to himself. He just wanted to do what he had to do and leave. He might never come back if he could get away clean.

"Where you been, Caleb? You know he been looking for you."

The sound of the old woman's voice startled him. She was there, sitting on her perch like she always was, her Sunday outfit covered by a thick black shroud with her head bowed as if in prayer. A stack of fans advertising Bedman's Funerary Services sat on her lap, waiting to be handed to the parishioners that would fill the sanctuary soon. Everything was the same as it always was inside the church where he had begged for forgiveness all those years ago, his knees bruised and bleeding. This Sunday morning was the same as every Sunday morning, yet the scene frightened Caleb to the core.

The old woman didn't look up when she spoke.

He passed by her without responding. There was nothing to say anyway.

He had been gone for—

"Hey doc, you almost done?"

"What?!?"

Dr. Lee nearly jumped out of his skin at the sound of his assistant's voice echoing in the room. That was one of the things he hated most about the autopsy rooms in that facility: the ceilings were so very high—state of the art diagnostic equipment advancement the culprit—that everything echoed. Sounds bouncing off the walls in the dead of night with nothing but one's self and a freezer full of the dead was disconcerting, even to someone who spent more time with those whose souls had left this earth than with those still living.

It didn't help that he had been reading a creepy story... reading a story when he was supposed to be writing his final notes... reading a book that he found in the deceased's possession.

He saw it on his desk when he sat down to fill out the last few lines on the autopsy report for one Megan Carlisle, age 28, cause of death: respiratory failure due to fire. There wasn't much to this case, at least not from his perspective. He wasn't the one who had to figure out why a young woman would set herself and her boyfriend on fire in her car in a public place, risking the lives of the other moviegoers. If the car had blown up... Dr. Lee didn't like to think that way. Two burning deaths were already two too many. Let the cops worry about the rest.

He sat down at his desk like he usually did, getting ready to finish up his part of the work on the case and then maybe take a minute to eat. It had been hours since he had, not since morning, when he'd had breakfast with his wife. He was famished. It always made him feel just the slightest bit guilty feeling hunger, in that place, but that's how he felt, nonetheless.

His eyes fell on the clear plastic bag that held the victim's belongings. There was nothing inside except a book. Nothing else survived the blaze. The car was consumed by flames; it took at least an hour to put out. The book shouldn't have made it out. It was old, nothing but brittle yellowed pages beneath a cover made of some kind of soft fabric. It should have gone up right away.

Someone said they saw her clutching the book to her chest while she burned...

Dr. Lee hadn't realized he had taken the book out of the

plastic bag until he felt the cover beneath his hand. Velvety soft.

Impossible.

He opened the cover and took in the smell, old and welcoming, nostalgic, though he couldn't figure out why. Not the smell of burn he had expected to catch, not the smell of flesh succumbing to flame.

He turned one page, and then another, seeing nothing but blankness, as though the fire had stripped away all of the ink, leaving barren pages in its wake. And then, the beginning of a story… the sound of voices singing, lifting above his head, carrying on the wind as they travelled up, up up.

"Dr. Lee," his assistant said, standing closer now. He had already gone out for lunch, the smell of onions floating heavily in the air before him, "you almost done? You should probably run out and grab something before… well, you know how it can get around here."

He did. One night they had four motorists come in right after a jumper and a stabbing victim. And contrary to what people might think, the dead won't wait.

"Right," Dr. Lee said distractedly. He put the book down reluctantly, wishing he could finish the story before he left, but knowing he would have no reason to give for even touching the book if someone asked. What could he possibly say… the story was so intriguing, he couldn't put it down? What reason could he supply for opening the book in the first place, or the bag besides? Fingerprints, residue, bodily secretions, whatever else the authorities might want to test the book for had been compromised because he couldn't control himself. But he had been drawn to it, hadn't he? Called to open the plastic, to stick his hand inside… to take a look.

Dr. Lee finished the last field on Megan Carlisle's autopsy

report, signed his name, and pushed himself away from the table. He picked up the book gingerly but quickly, holding it by the corners and thrusting it into the bag fast, before his assistant noticed, sealing it again and walking away as if he hadn't been holding it in his hands not a minute before. With a sigh, he left the office, the building, the book, finding food and eating it mirthlessly, the fragments of the story he was reading flashing in his mind, showing him things. Maybe he would finish it when he got back. Maybe he could hold the book back when the police came to talk to him about the victim. No one would believe it existed, not after a blaze like that. Maybe no one would remember that it was in her arms, fused to her breastbone so completely he had to use the rib cutter to get it out.

He heard singing off in the distance. Probably from the square, he thought as he walked back to the office, though it was a little late for that. The sound followed him, voices twisting, turning, intermingling with each other as they lamented their dirge.

The assistant felt restless. He paced the space he shared with the doctor, puttering around, looking for something to tidy, to clean, to do. The office was quiet with the doctor gone, and that was ok. He didn't mind the silence, even in a room filled with the dead. Some people got used to the job and some never did. Him? He came into it being ok with death. And he had seen a lot now, enough to have made someone hoping to wake up desensitized to it one morning quit and find a new career. Death was part of life, and he was there to help the process along as best he could.

Megan Carlisle's report was still lying on Dr. Lee's desk.

The man was brilliant but absentminded, and the assistant had taken to following behind him, dotting his i's and crossing his t's, and that was ok, too. He was fine being an assistant, didn't want his name to be the one on the report. They were a good team, and he wanted it to stay that way, even if it meant he had to clean up the doctor's messes every now and then.

Plastic shuffled as he picked up the report, pulling the corner from underneath what looked like a book. He picked it up, protected in the plastic bag, turning it over to inspect both sides.

"Where did this come from?" he said aloud to the empty room.

He didn't notice the air rushing out of the top of the bag, the seal breaking on its own as he held the book in his hands. He only saw, with distracted curiosity, that his hand was reaching inside to touch the velvety soft cover.

ACKNOWLEDGEMENTS

Thank you, Sean, Bree, and Mike, for helping me find pockets of time to do this thing I love. Thank you, Laura Fasching and MaryAnn David, for your keen eyes along this journey.

Thank you, readers, for travelling along this road with me.

ABOUT THE AUTHOR

L. Marie Wood is an award-winning psychological horror author and screenwriter. She won the Golden Stake Award for her novel *The Promise Keeper* and Best Horror, Best Short, and Best Afrofuturism/Horror/Sci-Fi screenplay awards at several film festivals.   An Active member of the HWA, Wood's short fiction has been published in *Slay: Stories of the Vampire Noire* and the Bram Stoker Finalist anthology, *Sycorax's Daughters.*   Learn more about her at www.l-mariewood.com or join the discussion on Twitter at @LMarieWood1 or on Facebook at www.facebook.com/LMarieWood.

ALSO BY L. MARIE WOOD

For Falstaff Books

The Lost Stories

Imitation of Life

At Mocha Memoirs

Telecommuting

The Black Hole

About Horror: The Study and The Craft

At Cedar Grove Publishing

Affinity Saga, Book One: The Tryst

Mars, the Band Man, and Sara Sue

The Promise Keeper

Crescendo

The Realm Trilogy

The Realm, Book 1

Cacophony, The Realm Book 2

Accursed, The Realm Book 3

FRIENDS OF FALSTAFF

Thank You to All our Falstaff Books Patrons, who get extra digital content each month! To be featured here and see what other great rewards we offer, go to www.patreon.com/falstaffbooks.

PATRONS